A

AN IDIOT'S

GUIDE TO

GETTING BY

To anyone who still has no idea what's going on. I feel your pain.

PROLOGUE

L iam hadn't planned on joining the 27 club, but locked in a house with a violent psychopath, it was beginning to look inevitable.

From his dusty hiding space under an old wooden bed he had to admit the guy was probably justified. There was no talking his way out of this one. Talking caused this whole mess. Angering the man was unintentional. Liam had inadvertently, but also quite deliberately, ruined his life. He wasn't usually one to cause upset. Liam barely strung together enough words to fill a sentence, let alone a person with rage. Lately, he had been a little lax on this credo.

His lips mouthed a silent prayer that the moth-eaten duvet covered him enough to give him a chance of making it out alive. Hope dwindled as soft footsteps passed outside the door. Fear only partly clouded his thoughts, leaving him free to berate himself. Liam had heard that in the face of certain death, one's life flashes before their eyes. He wished that were so, as cowering under the covers Liam only saw the mistakes that led him there. If only he hadn't sent that email.

TIP #1

KEEP YOUR COOL

"Welcome to the real world, where so much is out of your control but losing control will do you no favors."

CHAPTER 1

*H*ere lies Liam Broci, a lovable waste of space. Surviving his parents, Liam was tolerated by friends whom he somewhat regretfully leaves behind. To his credit, most are pretty busy with their own lives so they should get over his death pretty quickly. With the exception of Stef - sweet, beautiful Stef - his dearest friend who could have been the mother of his children had he ever grown a pair and -

Liam's alarm cut through his internal monologue. Lifting the phone, he silenced the blaring but remained on his side. He was not the kind of man to tackle the world head-on. He didn't command attention, he didn't look adversity in the eye, and, more importantly, he never leapt out of bed.

Liam watched as the alarm on his phone blared again moments later. Moving only his thumb, he pressed the snooze and continued to stare at the screen. The time was eight twenty-five. Work began at nine. If he got up right then he could be showered and dressed in ten minutes and out the door in another three. He could even grab a donut on his eight minute trek and make it to his desk by nine; but that would require him to get up right then. Instead he lay there, mindlessly scrolling until eight fifty-one. Liam rolled off the bed and raced into the shower. The hot water washed away all traces of adrenaline, encouraging him to stay under the spray longer than he should have.

Despite his lethargy, Liam made it out of the door in record time. He stood on the doorstep and breathed in the day. It smelled ordinary. The sky may have been overcast, but he didn't need to look up to see it. Gray blanketed the city, fading all the colors and blending them into each other. His eyes settled on the canopy above a beauty supply shop. The bright yellow poking through the dismal air looked garish and out of place. He exhaled and stepped out.

The air was wet. Liam turned up his collar knowing an umbrella, had he even owned one, would be of no use. The water didn't drop so much as cling to the air. Getting damp was unavoidable at this time of year. Words like dreary were better suited to cozier places like England. Misery in Europe is part of the appeal. There was nothing charming about autumn in Chicago. The sting of the wind watered his eyes. Not only was the air wet, it hurt too.

In an effort to perk himself up, Liam prolonged his journey with a shortcut through a donut shop. Standing at the counter was an authoritative looking woman who wore an outfit and expression that screamed "I've got a complicated order." Not one for keeping up with trends, Liam couldn't accurately describe her clothing, but from them he was certain that she made a habit of calling for the manager.

"Do you have gluten-free donuts?" Her voice sounded exactly how Liam imagined.

"No, ma'am. I'm afraid we don't serve those at this time." The cashier had a carefully practiced tone that suggested she worked in customer service for a while.

"Well do you know when you'll start?"

"No, ma'am."

Liam averted his gaze as the woman looked back, dramatically rolling her eyes. Fuck punctuality. He wanted to see how long it would take for this woman to lose her cool. He looked up just in time to lock eyes with the cashier who seemed apologetic. He shrugged in return.

"Fine," the woman continued, "which ones are fresh? I don't want any stale leftovers from yesterday."

"Ma'am, we just opened; they're all fresh."

In spite of her best efforts, exasperation seeped into her voice. *Tsk*, Liam thought stifling a smirk, *she's barely gotten started. That poor girl is going to need more stamina.*

"I don't appreciate your tone, but whatever. Give me half a dozen glazed, half a dozen chocolate frosted, three vanilla frosted with chocolate sprinkles, two pink with sprinkles, one with cinnamon sugar, three with powdered sugar, two sour cream and one jelly donut."

The girl behind the counter turned to fill two boxes with the order.

"Oh, and could I get the PB&J but with strawberry jelly instead of grape?"

The girl behind the counter started to explain the last request wasn't possible. For the sake of time, he was glad the woman took little convincing, but he was miffed at being denied an anecdote. Liam couldn't find it in his heart to be angry at someone so entertaining. The girl turned back to fill out the order. No sooner had she reached the first donut was she called back to the register.

"Wait, I forgot the coffees!"

The shop echoed with the collective groans of customers Liam hadn't noticed accumulated behind him. The woman shot a dirty look over her shoulder and continued.

"Three americanos, leave room for milk in one of them, four cappuccinos, dust two of them with chocolate powder, one mocha and four lattes: one hazelnut, two vanilla and one caramel."

"What sizes?"

"Let me check."

Fading red hair materialized out of the back room. A tall woman stumbled behind the now visibly frustrated cashier. She wore the same yellow polo as the cashier, with the addition of the word 'manager' on her name tag. Dark circles stood out against her pale skin. Liam wrongly remembered her with freckles and was surprised a few times a week to find none.

By the time he made it to the counter she had taken over the register. She had a perpetually bored look to her. Liam liked that about her. Her attempt to hand the difficult customer her receipt went ignored, so the paper lay abandoned by the metal bin on the counter. She stretched her neck, revealing a mermaid inked along the left side.

Pulling out his wallet, Liam joked, "I don't know if I followed the call of your neck or the sugar."

"Huh?"

The little pride he had in his clever joke quickly drained from his face. He was relieved to find her confused rather than disgusted. She probably wasn't expecting any words unrelated to the menu so she didn't process his attempt at humor.

"I meant…because of your tattoo. Like a siren song? But no, really, I'd just like a donut. A chocolate frosted one."

She nodded along to his babbling then reached for the sweet treat. Behind her back, Liam shook his head as if to erase the exchange. Had he spoken slower it could almost have been charming. Liam averted his eyes as he paid. He should know better than to flirt that early in the morning.

***

With all sense of self-preservation lost, a warm donut warmed his hand when Liam strode into the office at half past nine. Ignoring the disapproving glare of Lauren, his desk neighbor, he took his seat content to find that neither of his bosses had arrived. His laptop had barely reached a forty five degree angle when Lauren's short hair bobbed into his cubicle. Liam chewed slowly, drowning out her complaints of his tardiness with the sound of pastry turning into pulp in his mouth. Swallowing softly, Liam considered how rude it would be to take another bite.

Lauren worked in the sales department of Franklin Cooper Insurance. Granted, there were a number of factors that could affect her work: faulty telephones, poor internet connection, lack of cooperation from teammates, for example. However, save from personal interference with her work station, as in the in-house copywriter, there was nothing Liam could do to affect her work, and he made a point of avoiding her station and person at all times.

There was an ongoing misunderstanding regarding Liam's actual position in the company. He blamed it on the time, six months ago, when he was young and stupid enough to volunteer his services for things he wouldn't get paid for and set up the system for a multi-way conference call. It also might have been the many times he stupidly offered to help out with some basic tech problems. Since then, he was often called on to provide technical assistance, which made him reach two possible conclusions: either no one really knows what copywriter is, or they are well aware but can't be bothered to call I.T. with him sitting right there.

Lauren's long mustard colored nails gripped the back of his chair, so ignoring her was no longer an option. He didn't feel like having this argument again, so Liam dragged himself to her computer where it quickly became clear that she should not have graduated beyond a typewriter. He felt her breath on his ear as she whined about a spacing issue in her document. Liam removed a page break in a few short clicks which did nothing to lessen her annoyance. Excusing himself, he left her to stew.

Liam didn't do work friends, but Lauren had come close. When he first joined FCI, Lauren started off friendly. She went out of her way to make Liam feel included in the female-dominant office. She was a little chatty but unoffensive, and made a point of keeping Liam abreast of the office politics. About a year in, friendly turned too friendly. Out of nowhere, she had undergone a change in style and approach. Before he could process it, she went from complimenting his hazel eyes to fingering his dark curls as she passed. He hoped that a lack of eye contact and a haircut would be a sufficient deterrent. But a particularly hands-on encounter by the coffee machine led him to human resources. The semantics of harassment were debated over an exhausting couple of hours. The conclusion that Lauren's actions were not overtly sexual was disappointing. The jokes that he should have enjoyed the attention were infuriating. Liam never enjoyed receiving attention of any sort. His back had suffered from the tension he carried. Stef had noticed and was disgusted when he came clean in an effort to convince her to accompany him to the office Christmas party.

While they had a few drinks to get into a jolly mood beforehand; the pair made a beeline for the bar immediately upon entry. They barely had time to get comfortable before Lauren came to burst their boozy bubble.

"Hey, I'm Lauren," she giggled, "I'm basically Liam's work wife."

Though not particularly tall, Stef stood slightly above average height for a woman and towered over the barely five foot Lauren. Stef set down her glass and faced Lauren with a stare that could stop a bullet.

"So you're the grabby little bitch?"

Stifling a laugh, Liam led Stef away from the party, missing Lauren's reaction altogether. That memory warmed him whenever dealing with Lauren who got noticeably frosty towards him.

Back at his desk, Liam shuffled around in his bag. Personal items never made it onto his desk for the same reason he didn't hang around the break room — he actively avoided making small talk. There was one exception. A wooden frame, smaller than a postcard, kept lidded most of the time, that held an aging photograph of a smiling couple on their wedding day. Opening the frame, his eyes ignored the man, whose familiarity was limited to the features he saw in the mirror. Gently he glided his thumb over his mother's face. Her face had held that same roundness. Her hair was longer than he got used to seeing, but he'd take what he could get. The pain of her passing wasn't fresh, but as much as he missed her, Liam found some solace in the thought his parents were reunited.

He turned back to his computer and set about his usual routine of rooting between checking emails, monitoring the on-going projects, and following up on responses to his submissions. For the most part, Liam spent his days amending engagement letters and occasionally preparing promotional materials to include in proposals for services. Those have been rare, which made him wonder about the state of the company. It wasn't enough to worry him since he maintained that he would jump ship at the first chance he got.

***

Liam managed to enjoy a couple of peaceful hours before the bosses arrived, bellowing for attention. As a small company, the firm was owned and managed by a married pair of assholes. It was beyond the realm of understanding how people could get themselves into positions of power without the ability to turn on a computer without assistance. And yet, it was their first demand of the day. Fortunately, the actual I.T. department was called to set them up for the day, giving Liam time to sit back and work on the closest thing he had to a passion. Unable to afford therapy on his own, since the work sponsored insurance didn't cover it, Liam developed a way to cope with the monotony and aggravations of the day by drafting short poems and sending them to Stef for her amusement. This could fill only so much time before he tuned in to the ticking of the clock, which got unnervingly louder.

The hairs on the back of his neck spiked at the realization that sound came from high heels on linoleum. Those impatient steps were unique to his boss Sarah Franklin, who was fast approaching. Sarah could go from show horse to untamed mare in record time. Employees of FCI learned to use her pace to gage her mood. Soft and leisurely meant she was feeling pleasant, perhaps even sociable. On those occasions, she would take her time making the rounds at the desks on her way to her office. A gallop meant someone's head was bound to be bitten off.

"Liam, come," she barked.

He didn't appreciate being summoned like a dog, but droopingly obliged.

"Close the door."

He felt his stomach drop ten stories, but he schooled his features as he took a seat.

"We have to go over the format of your proposals. The last one you sent was abysmal."

"How so?" He hoped his voice came out even so as not to give her any sign she was already getting to him.

"The entire thing was completely off. It read wrong and there were so many grammatical errors."

Liam clenched his jaw. He may not have liked his job, but he delivered good work. He wasn't in the mood to take her destructive criticism.

"Can you give me examples?"

Sarah narrowed her eyes then turned her monitor to face him.

"See? There."

In the copy Liam prepared concerning life insurance, Sarah pointed to a single highlighted word.

"You should have said 'security' not 'protection.' Not only does it sound better, but it's what we're selling. And there! You should have put a comma there. Now that whole sentence reads wrong."

Liam pinched the bridge of his nose. His plan to remain unfazed was all too quickly abandoned. He now knew who gave a fuck about the Oxford comma. Looking closely at the monitor, Liam saw the root of the issue. The prospective client passed on their latest proposal and Sarah had never learned how to handle rejection. She needed to lash out, and that day Liam wore a target on his back.

"When we brought you on to this team we assumed a big risk. But with your track record you looked like you could deliver results and I'm just not seeing them," she said in a syrupy voice. She widened her eyes in a way she probably thought was cute but made Liam wrinkle his nose. He furiously tapped his finger on his thigh.

"Have the number of responses decreased during my time here?"

"No," she looked taken aback. "Actually the opposite."

"So they increased? And you're upset," he sneered.

Sarah shook her head. "The numbers are steady."

Liam waited, but she offered no explanation. He threw up his hands. "I'm not seeing the problem here."

Sarah rested her arms on her desk. "We know you are capable of more, but you demonstrate a lack of enthusiasm that doesn't bode well for your future here."

Liam took a deep breath. Processing the events of the last five minutes was proving difficult.

"Have you anything to say for yourself?"

"About complying with the terms of my job description? I'm going to need a minute to think of something."

"You have to understand that sending out work like this is unacceptable." Condescension laced her every word. "Your work is a reflection of us. How do you think this makes us look?"

The inside of his mouth was cut up from biting back comments. He physically couldn't hold back for much longer.

"You mean sending out copy in the format you designed, revised, and confirmed?"

He was toeing the line but took pleasure in watching her beady eyes bulge out of her head. Underneath her hooked nose, the way she opened and closed her mouth strengthened her birdlike features.

"I never saw this," she raised her voice with indignation. Her naturally nasal voice was shrill. Liam noted that after reaching a certain octave it became harder for her to mask her disdain.

"You sent it."

"Why would I send a proposal when that's your

"Because you told me you wanted to send this one directly."

Tilting her head back to look down at him, she spat, "I did no such thing."

Liam leaned forward and angled the monitor back to her. At the top of the screen he pointed at her email in the outgoing address box. Her nostrils flared but she didn't meet his eyes. The phone interrupted their standoff. She roughly lifted the headpiece and Liam took his leave,

"We'll go over your formatting later."

Liam nodded and left her office. He made a mental note to ask Stef for her chiropractor's details as a stretch loosened several loud clicks along his spine. Plopping into his chair, Liam swiveled into place and went back to work.

Approximately twenty minutes later, he heard the clacks of Sarah's shoes announcing her departure for lunch. He decided to follow her example and run away for a bit.

An hour later, Liam returned to find the aggravated mistress of the office hadn't returned. In her place, she left her complacent husband Peter Cooper. Liam groaned when he spotted Peter hovering around his desk.

"Oh, Liam, can we have a word when you get a minute?"

Liam nodded and followed Peter into his office. In stark contrast to his wife, Peter moved at the pace of an aging sheep dog. He took his seat and leaned back before sluggishly spouting off a sermon about being present and available to the other colleagues. Peter delivered his speech to the wall over Liam's shoulder, occasionally waving around a pen for emphasis.

"So I can't leave for lunch," Liam asked in a clipped manner.

Peter shifted in his seat. "That's not what I'm saying."

"Then what's the issue?"

Peter sat up and faced his irate employee. "There have been complaints about your tardiness."

"From whom?"

Peter was not a photogenic man and confusion really emphasized that about him.

"That's not important," he said dismissing the point with a wave.

"Can I guess?" While his lunch break gave him some time to cool off, it did not replenish any of the patience he lost earlier. He had reached his limit of stupid interactions for the day.

"I'd rather you didn't."

"Yeah, but does she have an upturned nose, trouble minding her own business and a name that rhymes with Snore-an?"

Peter tried hard to look unamused. "That's beside the point. Sarah has also expressed concern with your performance lately."

Liam scoffed. He doubted she was capable of concern.

Peter continued. "I've also noticed that some of the computers have been running a bit slow." Peering over his rectangular frames he added, "I think they are in need of updating."

Looking as though he was sucking on a lemon, Liam nodded slowly. "I'll pass that on to the I.T. Department."

Peter puffed out his chest. He got touchy when he assumed that people were making fun of him; an assumption he often made correctly. It wasn't that he was entirely humorless. After years of not being in on the joke, he seemed to take issue with them altogether.

"Because I'll pass them on the way to the coffee machine," Liam continued tentatively, "I'll need a caffeine fix before I get back to writing copy." Noting the persisting look of puzzlement on Peter's face Liam exhaled deeply. "Because I'm the copywriter." He hoped that was enough to clarify the situation.

"Ah," Peter flipped through pages in the notepad in front of him, "yes, of course." His voice sounded unconvinced, but Liam thought it best not to press the issue. Peter skimmed along a page, searching for his next point. Closing the book once more, he looked back up at Liam. "Basically we want to see more effort from you."

Liam rubbed the back of his neck. He felt the blood pounding in his ears. All his muscles tensed. Oblivious, Peter continued. "Just show us you want to be here."

Liam realized that Peter had likely prepared this speech based on the little he could make out of his wife's vitriol. It came off like he just adopted a spiel he used to inspire the sales team. It wasn't having the same effect on Liam who hadn't been inspired in years.

After one too many unpaid internships and unrealistic exceptions for his social media presence resulted in him giving up in a career in journalism, Liam had settled for going through the motions of getting a steady paycheck. As long as he could make use of his way with words and skills he picked up in school, Liam could excuse it as not selling out. Factoring in his crushing debt, Liam calculated the cost of his boredom divided by the price of dealing with unhinged employers and intolerable colleagues and found his paycheck wanting.

"Are we agreed?"

Liam had zoned out a while ago. He knew that he'd been asked a question so he searched Peter's face for a clue on how to respond. Usually he'd nod and move along, but he wasn't confident that agreeing to anything was a safe option at this point.

"Sorry, what?"

"You'll rework this new proposal for today and apologize to Sarah when she gets back."

Liam blinked a few times. He hoped that would reboot his brain for, at that moment, nothing but an error screen appeared before him. He couldn't find the path used to reach that convoluted conclusion and all desire to try escaped him. His head felt heavy. Liam was suddenly aware of his aching body. He felt like he'd been carrying a hefty load, though he spent most of his days seated. He was worn out. At only twenty six, Liam was exhausted.

We were not made to suffer.

His mother's voice rang out in his head. He wanted desperately to agree with her, but life was proving otherwise. His solution was simple: apologize, keep his head down and continue dredging on. As he opened his mouth to speak, he could see his mother's disappointed face and his throat dried up. Liam barely heard the words he said over the sound of his heartbeat.

"Is quitting an option?"

Peter nodded before the realization hit. "Wait, what?"

"Because I do."

"Let's not be hasty. This was all just a misunderstanding."

"Except that it's not." Liam didn't have the energy to argue. "It's not just today and it's not just her. I'm done here."

Peter wiped his brow. "Why don't you sleep on it?" He reached for a glass of water and took a swig only to find it empty. "I mean, you're going to have to talk to Sarah about this," he said staring down the empty glass. "She's the one that processes these things."

Liam narrowed his eyes at him. A part of him wanted to remind the man that he also owned the company, but a much greater part couldn't be bothered.

"Just, just sleep on it. We'll all talk tomorrow."

Liam shrugged and left. He made no effort to hide his anger. He hadn't realized that his frustration had been building to this point. It had been a whole year of this: vicious gossips, being talked down to, and impromptu tribunals where the defense never mattered. Liam wasn't sure what he had expected of the corporate life, but it certainly wasn't more high school.

Settling back in his chair, Liam started his email to Stef. In the body he summarized his day in two poems.

A haiku for the boss
  A cunt is a cunt.
  That is undeniable.
  But she takes the cake.

CHAPTER 1

A limerick for her mate
  At FCI there is a terrible dullard
  who lives his life as a complete coward
  to his bitch of a wife
  he signed over his life
  and castrated himself for an iota of power.

At five past five, Liam sent off his work and performed his end of day routine. He checked the calendar and to-do list, checking off what he could. He saved the open documents and shut down the machine before returning his notebook, pens, and picture frame to his bag. Throwing it over his shoulder, Liam kneed his chair into place and legged it to the door. In his periphery, he saw Lauren grab her things so he promptly put on his headphones. He didn't bother to turn on any music. Liam made it into the elevator before Lauren could get to the door. He felt no remorse for ignoring her faint cries to hold the elevator.

CHAPTER 2

L iam was shaken awake as his phone vibrated somewhere on his bed. He aimed for the snooze button, but shot upright when a disembodied voice called out.

"You up?"

Stef's voice came through breathy and muffled as though half of her face were hidden in a pillow. Liam sighed deeply recognizing her voice. He rubbed his eyes and mumbled some form of agreement.

"Good," she said, "there's time for breakfast. See you in twenty."

Groggily, he accepted and threw himself back on the pillow. With phone already in hand, Liam turned onto his side and promptly started his morning by procrastinating. His brow furrowed at the record number of notifications. There were fifteen messages from colleagues, forty-nine emails from work and three new tweets tagging him. He started with the work emails, which seemed more urgent due to the sheer number of them. His heart dropped when he saw that most of the emails were sent in reply to him. The blood drained from his face. He didn't need to see the original message to know that the office was reacting to his creative outburst. In his rush to leave, he must have blindly accepted the first suggestion after putting in "*st.*" Instead of addressing Stef, he sent his unfiltered opinions of his bosses to the entire staff.

Here lies Liam Broci, an absolute idiot who called his boss a cunt and copied the entire office. Aged twenty-six in body and eighty-six in spirit, Liam passed, surprisingly not from the embarrassment of making such a monumental cockup, but from starvation due to sudden unemployment and a depressing lack of funds.

Had he been capable of movement, Liam would have facepalmed himself. The shock wore off unnaturally quickly and Liam accepted his fate with undue grace. He had been wanting to quit for a while and had even expressed it to management. He figured that, given the circumstances, no one would mind if he simply didn't return. For the first time in longer than he'd care to admit, Liam felt no need to procrastinate. Getting ready was a breeze.

In no time, he was sitting at the diner around the corner from his apartment waiting for Stef. A blur of all black passed the window. Upon entering the establishment, Stef removed her hat and smoothed her hair which, in spite of the ridges and coils caused by her tight curls, was always neatly pinned back. She made her way over to their usual spot and maneuvered her long legs into the booth across from Liam, blowing a kiss in his general direction. Meeting for breakfast before work wasn't uncommon since they were practically neighbors. It simply hadn't happened often as of late as Liam could rarely find the will to get up in the mornings. He would try to make the effort when she asked to catch up and she compromised on meeting over breakfast instead of in crowded bars.

***

When English literature major Liam met pre-law candidate Stef in the dorms during their first year of undergrad at Northwestern, she was using her trust fund to cover living costs, while her parents took care of the tuition. Stef was an only child in an affluent family. No excuse was too flimsy to celebrate her existence. Stef went on to get a Masters in law and had plans of pursuing a life in academia by returning for a doctorate before a falling out with her parents and overnight notoriety put those plans on hold roughly three years prior. Since then, Stef had liquidated the remainder of her trust to cover daily expenses while she turned her yoga hobby into a source of income.

***

A waitress dropped off a cup of tea in front of Stef and poured out some fresh coffee for Liam before leaving them to talk. Stef started them off while she customized her brew with just enough milk to match her skin tone. She let the sugar flow freely into her mug before sliding it to Liam and stirred vigorously all the while never stopping for a breath. Liam suppressed a smirk at how an endless string of tangents made their way into her stories. Stef held an impressive array of facts which prompted her nickname of 'professor'. Finally completing her recap, Stef rewarded herself with a sip. Liam watched her eyes flutter at the first taste and chose that moment to announce his sudden retirement from FCI. Stef's eyes widened for a moment. She gently paced her cup back on its saucer and looked back at him.

"Explain."

So he did. She listened courteously. Her expressive eyebrows followed along with his story, while her attentive lips moved to the right as she was known to do when thinking. All the while she remained silent.

"Comments?"

Stef shook her head. She lifted her cup to continue drinking. Liam searched her dark eyes for a sign of anything resembling disappointment or judgement. Liam couldn't help but worry about her reaction to the news. Despite her straightforward nature, she didn't have a malicious bone in her body. Still, he was curious to see how she'd respond to the details surrounding his departure. He relaxed when his search proved fruitless.

"I guess this means you're free today."

Liam nodded.

"Would you mind stopping by my apartment for a bit?" Her soft voice was always a treat, but the tinge of amusement intrigued him. He raised an eyebrow in response.

"I've got a package arriving sometime this afternoon, and I've picked up an extra shift."

TIP #2

SET A HEALTHY WORK/LIFE BALANCE

"Remember you work to live, not the other way around. Get a hobby and associate with non-work related people."

CHAPTER 3

A ndrija needed to get a proper job. Something with regular work hours, health insurance, and fewer psychos. It wasn't that he was sick of his current job. It had everything: flexible schedule, good salary, and, more importantly, he excelled at it. He just wanted the option of turning down assignments without the fear of getting shot in the head. Not that the mob did much of that anymore. Recruiting was increasingly difficult and, contrary to popular belief, mobsters weren't savages; though that wasn't an image they were looking to change. They just liked obedience and put in the effort to ensure it.

Andy joined the Serbian mafia two days shy of his thirteenth birthday. Trading an unstable home for a bit of grunt work was a no-brainer. Through the years, he was given every opportunity to climb the ranks, so at thirty-two he was respected and feared. At least he thought he was until he answered the call to babysit two new recruits. Technically, one new recruit and one transfer. Andy didn't want to think about what it meant that he was assigned to this task.

Their first stop was a convenience store that subscribed to their insurance plan. They took pride in delivering face-to-face service. The owner was a skittish man who immediately set about pouring them some coffee. Andy took his with a nod, appreciating his initiative. He didn't expect to see much of it from his companions. He hadn't had a chance to know them and he would have preferred to keep it that way. The younger one didn't look old enough to vote so Andy dismissed him entirely. The transfer on the other hand.

Vincent Petrović reminded Andy of dark beer. He was stout, top heavy, and foaming at the mouth. One whiff was enough to determine that he could stand to take better care of himself. Vince bathed in cologne like he never heard of running water. The way he stuffed himself into his clothes repulsed Andy. He didn't care what size a person was so long as they dressed properly. He pressed his lips together as he took in Vince's disheveled clothing as though he dressed straight out of his suitcase. Andy was determined to tolerate all of this if he didn't already hate him. Andy didn't like people who make themselves so comfortable too early. After being slapped on the back by Vince's meaty palm as he laughed at his own tasteless jokes for the second time in ten minutes, Andy was certain he did not care for Vince. All of his efforts to steer the conversation back to work went ignored. Vince showed no interest in quietly learning the ropes. The longer this interaction when on, the more sure Andy became that Vince couldn't do anything quietly. That was a liability.

Vince slung a burly arm over the young one, whose name Andy still hadn't bothered to get, and began to regale them with stories neither had requested, which Andy quickly tuned out. Very little of what other people said interested him, much less when the topic of conversation was themselves. The hubris dripping from Vince's tongue rendered his words superfluous. He was full of shit. Giving him an audience would only encourage that. Vince took no notice of his colleague's disinterest and continued running his mouth. Apparently he didn't require participation to carry on a conversation. Andy checked his watch as Vince began a soliloquy about his conquests back east. He was disappointed to find that he had only managed to tune out for a minute. In that time, the conversation had taken a darker tone.

"You see, we'd get these big ass fires going, right? Then we'd sit the motherfucker close by."

This piqued Andy's interest, against his better judgement.

"At this point he can't see shit cause we still got him blindfolded. But he can feel the heat on his back." Vince let out a hearty laugh. "We get the fucker sweating in more ways than one. That's when we - "

A cold gust hit them as the door swung open. Andy barked an order for

21

silence. Finally the man had something interesting to say, but Andy couldn't risk Vince continuing when some dude walked in. Vince grunted at Andy then turned his attention to the intruder. While the kid slunk against the counter, both Andy and Vince tracked the customer's path through the store. He, in turn, paid the three no mind and mouthed along to whatever song came through his headphones. Content that they wouldn't be overheard, Vince continued.

"Where was I?"

"Fire," the kid replied.

"Right, yeah. So we remove the blindfold and the bastard is facing the wall. We're all behind him so he can only see our shadows."

"How philosophical," Andy quipped mirthlessly.

Vince faced Andy; his already squashed face scrunched further.

"Like Plato and the cave," Andy explained.

"How the fuck should I know what that fag did in caves?"

Andy stonily disregarded that comment. Clearly Vince could only respond to confusion with anger. It amused him to think that Vince must always be angry.

"Anyway, that's when we start the questions. Every wrong answer gets a burn right on his feet."

The customer pushed past them and dumped his groceries on the counter. Andy scoffed at his selection. Cereal, canned tuna, sliced bread, and a carton of milk. Vince carried on talking without a care. *His meals were probably worse*, thought Andy. Turning his attention back to the interrupter, Andy made no effort to hide his analysis. Dark hair wildly peeked out from his beanie. Faint stubble dotted his weak jaw which clenched momentarily before he resumed his bopping. All the while the man kept his eyes stained firmly on the counter. He wasn't as young as Andy initially assumed. The man's terrible posture took a few years off, but he was clearly a grown man. It was difficult to discern his exact height from the way he slouched, but Andy figured he came up just short of his own six feet and one inch. His body was well hidden by an oversized jacket that reached past his knees. It looked expensive, but was not tailored to fit properly. He made a valiant attempt to fill it out, likely with the help of additional layers. Still, the jacket hung a little loose. Andy lost interest in the man somewhere around his scuffed black boots. He turned back to Vince's story.

"Once we're satisfied, the guy gets shot then strung up."

Vince took a proud sip of his, now cold, coffee to celebrate the end of his story. The young guy fidgeted in place. His eyebrows furrowed with dissatisfaction.

"Why?"

"The fuck you mean 'why'?" Vince asked, raising his voice.

"Why go to the effort of hanging a guy after he's been shot? Why not just dump him somewhere?"

Andy raised his eyebrows in acknowledgment.

"Because," Vince hesitated for just a second too long earning Andy's full attention once again. "It sends a message."

"What message?"

"That they're a rat." Vince reached over and smacked the kid over the head. "You've got a lot to learn."

So do you, Andy thought. He doubted that Vince had ever participated in an interrogation like the one he had just described. Looking closely, Andy doubted that Vince had even held a gun before. Andy looked up into the mirror behind the counter and locked eyes with the customer just as he was paying. He saw a flash of fear before the man grabbed his things and ran out. He shook his head as Vince launched into another story. Not only was he an idiot, but he was a careless idiot. That type is more trouble than they are worth.

He had heard scattered details about Vince's ventures in the family business. When news of his failures reached the midwest, the majority of his colleagues were eager to meet the New York fuck-up. Andy, on the other hand, was content to laugh at his misfortunes behind his back. This association would not bode well. He could only pray this wouldn't come back to bite him.

Our Father who art in Heaven,

Forgive us our trespasses, as we forgive those who trespass against us; and lead us not into the temptation to smash this moron's head in.

Andy had neither the time nor patience to tolerate Vince for another second. Without a word, he pulled on his coat and strode out. The other two scrambled after him. Dismissing them with a nod, Andy headed downtown alone.

CHAPTER 4

The sun dried the pavement, dampened from that morning's drizzle. It did nothing to fix the biting cold. Andy kept his head down and weaved between the pedestrians that littered the sidewalk. He stopped at an ATM and withdrew a hefty wad of cash. Andy darted in and out of buildings, ensuring he would not be followed. Once certain he'd lost any potential tails, he headed to his destination.

The motel ahead was off-white, worn out from pollution and age. It's gaudy red doors stood out. Even in its heyday, it was never an elegant establishment, but time had been particularly unkind. Around the side of the building, Andy headed up a stairwell looking for some reprieve from the cold.

Standing just out of sight between two floors stood a pale dark-haired beauty. Her shoes made it clear that she had no place there. Her long hair swung with her pacing. The large buttons of her coat reflected the light as she turned. It hung open, giving Andy a quick glimpse of the figure-hugging outfit she wore underneath. He stayed back and admired her a moment longer, enjoying her obvious discomfort in the location. She reached into her pocket for a phone. At this, he snuck up behind her and removed it from her hand.

"No phones."

"Andrija," she purred.

He returned the phone to her coat and led her up the remaining stairs, down the hall a couple of doors, into the room he rented earlier that day. Behind the closed door, Andy wrapped an arm around her waist and a hand around her neck. He pressed his lips hard to hers. It was a greeting reserved for more than mere acquaintances. Mischa Mirković was a former ballerina turned gangster's trophy wife. This wouldn't be a problem if Andy were the mobster in question. Or, at the very least, if her husband wasn't Andy's boss.

Andy could trust Mischa to keep her mouth shut. Such a pretty mouth it was, resting in a sullen pout. Crossing her husband meant certain death so Andy felt no need to double down on the threats. It made seducing her so much easier. All he really had to do was keep quiet while she vented. On occasion, he'd even extend her the courtesy of listening. Her move from repressed childhood into her ancient husband's bed left her wanting. Andy had to do little more than exist to get her blood pumping. She hardly seemed to mind the dodgy motels if it meant she'd be allowed to orgasm too.

Mischa broke the kiss and moved deeper into the room. She shed her outer layers and threw them haphazardly on a chair in the corner.

"This week was a nightmare."

Their meetings always started the same. The beauty would unload her frustrations towards her husband which Andy would quietly absorb. On occasion she let slip useful tidbits, but not often enough to make these visits more regular. Sometimes Andy had considered using her for information, but as her cream blouse slid off her shoulders, he remembered how he wanted to use her.

"We should run away."

As usual, Mischa broke the silence with romantic notions Andy would tactfully dismiss. He laid his jacket carefully on the round table. "How would we live?"

"We could rob a bank." Hope brightened her blue eyes. "Like Bonnie and Clyde!"

Andy pulled her flush against him and kissed her hard again, this time to erase her stupidity. She melted into him. By the time they broke apart, she had quieted significantly.

"I think he is having me followed," she whispered into his neck. "Can you believe that? How could he not trust me?"

She turned to the windows beside them. She pressed herself against the wall and softly moved the curtain aside to look through a small gap as she described the labyrinth she took to get there. Andy felt this was as good a time as any to wind down the talking portion of the afternoon. One of his arms found its former place around her waist while a more liberal hand snaked its way into her bra. He kissed her temple and whispered into her ear. "Do you want me to kill him?"

Andy could see the tiny bumps on her skin lift in response to his proximity. He pressed harder against her. She bit her lip loosely, allowing a whimper to escape. He smirked against her skin. He loved having this effect on her. In the middle of a tacky room, sweetly whispering murderous thoughts, Andy knew how to sweep a girl onto her knees.

Half wrapped in the sheets, Andy stared at the ceiling trying not to think about the last time this room got a proper cleaning. The shower went quiet. Andy couldn't understand how she could wash in there. He didn't envy her choices: shower in that disgusting bathroom or return home smelling of another man. Andy kept his eyes fixed on the ceiling, when she emerged, not feeling up for round three. She curled into the nook of his arm. He felt the towel she had wrapped herself in scratch at his torso. She dreamed loudly of the life they could have. He remained still.

"Andy, do you love me?"

He closed his eyes so she wouldn't see him roll them.

"Of course, petal."

"Why don't you ever say it?"

Andy turned his head to face her. She had washed away all her makeup but the plump apples of her cheeks stayed rosy. Tenderly, he traced them with a finger. "Does everything need to be said out loud?"

"It would be nice to hear you say it."

Andy scanned the room for a way out of this conversation. He sat up, pulling away from her.

"I thought you knew me better than that."

Andy felt the mattress dip behind him. Her arms circled his waist and she rested her forehead between his shoulder blades. "That's not how I meant it," she said, sounding small.

"Words are nothing, you should know this." Andy caressed her hand. "We are surrounded by liars, murderers and thieves. We are liars by being here." He dropped his hands to the edge of the bed. "Words mean nothing. Look at actions. Have I ever hurt you?" he asked, looking into her teary eyes.

"No."

"Do I make you happy?"

"Yes."

He had her now.

"Then what more do you need to know?"

"The future."

Shit. He should have quit when he was ahead. With a sigh, he fought the urge to dive for his trousers and run out the door. Instead he grabbed her hands and traced across them with his thumbs.

"I can't tell you that," he said softly. He softened his features expertly as he looked deep into her eyes. He'd never seen her so serious.

"I need to know what will happen with us. We can't do this everyday and it's always too long until the next time. I don't want to go back to him."

Andy looked away but she turned his sculpted face back to her. "I'm serious, Andrija. We can't do this forever. I want more."

He swallowed a groan. This wasn't his first dalliance with a married woman. He hoped that their prior commitments meant he wouldn't have to have this discussion. But there he was, sitting face to face with the wife of the most dangerous man in the city. The ball may have been in his court, but his balls were in her hands. He needed to break this to her gently. Andy couldn't risk her going home and fucking things up for him. Distraction was his only option. He kissed her more chastely this time. She chased his mouth as he withdrew. Gingerly, he cradled her face.

"There is no future for us in Chicago," his voice was barely audible. He knew the last two words were superfluous, but they provided just enough ambiguity to give her hope. She violently attached her face to his, kissing up his hairline. By the time she figured out his true meaning, Andy hoped he'd be long gone.

***

An hour later, Andy washed away his indiscretions in his shower. Lathering his skin, he took inventory of the bruises forming. He should feel something. Regret. Remorse. Unclean. He pressed on the red mark at the base of his neck and let pain give way to pride. He stepped out of the shower and wrapped a towel around himself. HIs phone screen lit up with notifications. He meant to head down to the church, but the cross on his living room wall would have to suffice. Just as he knelt on the ground, his phone went off again. Andy shot it a look of disgust. It was his boss. Holding his breath, Andy answered.

"How'd it go today?" The voice was gravelly from age and power.

"All good, Nick." Andy kept his voice even. "Need something?"

"Yeah. Take Vince out tonight. Give that asshole a proper welcome." Nick laughed, "That little bastard's father keeps calling me to check on him."

Andy rubbed the back of his neck.

"What? You got plans tonight?" Nikola Mirković expected acknowledgment of his orders. Silence was never an acceptable answer.

"No, sir. I'll take him out."

"Good." Nick hung up at that.

Andy tossed his phone onto the armchair beside him and got up off the floor. He moved closer to the cross and rested his head on the wall beneath it. He wished he had said something. Even if he didn't have plans, he didn't appreciate being forced into babysitting that slovenly man-child. Andy sneered at the thought of Vince. That prick who never had to work a day in his life. Vince never had to drop anything at a moment's notice. He probably could turn all work down without breaking a sweat because he had a powerful daddy. Unlike Andy, who came from nowhere and risked it all by sleeping with his boss' wife. Resigned, he pushed off the wall and walked into his closet, continuing his prayer as he dressed. The fact he survived so long in this industry was a miracle. He requested another one to make it out.

TIP #3

DON'T COVET THY NEIGHBOR'S LIFE

"Window shopping sucks when you're broke. Just remember, they don't put the defective items on display."

CHAPTER 5

A month and a half had passed since his dramatic departure from FCI. Liam liked to imagine that it had caused a ruckus, but since he hadn't returned, he didn't get to see any of the fall out. In all likelihood, they went immediately back to business as usual. He didn't want to admit that thoroughly disappointed him.

At well past lunchtime, Liam rolled out of bed. Turning a deaf ear to his rumbling stomach, he grabbed his laptop and settled on his usual corner of the couch where the cushion had molded to the shape of his body. The computer opened to the browser he opened the night before. He hovered the mouse over the tabs of jobs he meant to apply for, but productivity eluded him. Liam scrolled through a true crime forum.

Recovering from his traumatic work experience required Liam to waste time around the house with gruesome articles, video games, and generally avoiding human contact. Initially, it was only meant to take a couple of days, but the lack of responses to his applications discouraged him. He quickly fell into a new routine. Everyday saw him wake up and lounge in bed until it got painful, get up and ignore the lack of food by avoiding the kitchen, turn on his laptop and skim job postings, fix a meager lunch with whatever was lying around, apply or one or two jobs while a gnawing hunger builds, relent and spend more on takeout than he should, stay up into the early hours gaming then crash in a half made bed. Rinse and repeat.

Liam reached the point in the schedule where he braved the kitchen only to find that his resources were finally depleted. Standing in front of the open cupboard, closely analyzing the spare contents which mostly consisted of condiments and plastic utensils, it dawned on him that he hadn't left the apartment in a while. Repeating his shopping list like a mantra, Liam popped on headphones and a jacket.

Across the street sat a most convenient store. Though the glass pane, Liam could see the shop owner moving around inside. Liam reached into his pocket to pause his music in order to greet him. The tight space was crowded with three other men, so he didn't bother to remove his headphones. One of them demanded silence when he entered. His knowledge of Balkan languages were filed away from disuse but he could still identify the man spoke in Serbian. Liam schooled his features to hide his discomfort and continued straight to the cereal aisle. As he reached for a bright blue box, the hairs on the back of his neck stood. He was being watched. Liam moved further into the aisle bobbing his head in time with an imaginary song. He didn't want to reach back into his pocket and he really didn't want them thinking he was paying them any attention. They didn't look like they'd appreciate being eavesdropped on. He angled away and their conversation resumed in English, seemingly content that Liam wasn't listening. Breathing deeply, he focused on keeping his face blank as the larger man gleefully described the process of burning the soles of his victim's feet, enthusiastically miming the process like a maestro.

Liam blindly grabbed the nearest items and rushed to pay. He kept his head down and tapped nervously on the counter. He paused for a moment then resumed, adding more bopping in the hopes they would assume he was still listening to music. As the cashier rang up his items, Liam glanced up into the mirror behind the counter. Curiosity got the better of him and he quickly studied their faces. He rationalized it was safer to commit their faces to memory.

Wide was the best way to describe the one talking. All of his features looked to have been stretched out. He was roughly Liam's height with far more girth around the middle. His head was rectangular and featured a prominent nose that looked as though some invisible force was pressing it down. He moved so quickly, it was hard to get a closer look. The tall one beside him stood eerily still. His similarities to a statue didn't end there. He must have been sculpted. His neatly maintained facial hair accentuated his strong jaw, while his unmistakably blow dried hair could do very little to hide the ears that poked out. Liam was aware of a third person, but didn't even bother to give them a once over. He couldn't look away from the tall man. There was something unnerving about his stillness. Liam's heart stopped when the statue made eye contact in the mirror. A cold blue stood out against the warm olive of his skin. Doused with dread, Liam scrambled to grab his items and change. He shot out of the store, praying they hadn't noticed which way he went. A loud ringing accompanied him across the street.

Back in his apartment, Liam hastily put his groceries away. He had forgotten more than half of the things he set out for, but he didn't care. He didn't want to stay there a second longer. The ringing got louder. A heavy knot formed in his stomach forcing him against the sink. A dull burning climbed in his chest. Hunched over, he gasped for air. Furiously pulling off his layers, Liam crashed onto the cold tiles. He sat in the crumpled heap of discarded clothes struggling to catch his breath, never taking his eyes off the front door. The voice of reason assuring him he wasn't in danger was drowned out by the hammering of his heart.

Here lies Liam Broci, murdered in his own apartment after a run-in with first class psychos at his neighborhood convenience store. By the grace of God, Liam was an insignificant speck, not worth getting their hands dirty over, so they merely shot him twice, execution style. We should take comfort that his last thought was that it could have been so much worse.

The haze let up just enough to allow him to stand. Liam made his way to the sofa onto which he flopped, face first, with all the grace of a hippo off a diving board. He ran both hands through his wild hair. He curled himself further, hoping to become one with the furniture. He had lived in that area for a few years without any close encounters of a criminal kind. It was impressive by Chicago standards. The story he overheard was bad enough, but the tall man frightened him to the core. That guy had definitely seen some things... or done them.

His appetite burned away with the image of sizzling feet. Burying himself in bed seemed like the only reasonable course of action. Liam headed to his bedroom, leaving his clothes strewn around the kitchen floor. There was very little a nap could actually fix, but it wouldn't make anything worse. He could always count on being unconscious to make him feel better.

None of the voices in his head got with the program. He tried a deep breathing technique Stef taught him. The humming in his head began to die down just as his pocket started vibrating. As he was weeks into screening his calls, Liam meant only to quickly glance at the name before tossing the phone to the end of his bed. Though still a little blurry, Liam could make out a picture of Stef.

"Professor?"

"Are you conscious?" Stef's voice was nearly washed out by the screams of children in the background. Liam managed some monosyllabic noise.

"Is that a no or an 'I wish I wasn't'?"

He smiled into his pillow then rolled onto his back. "What's up?"

"Just reminding you that we've got dinner with the twins tonight."

Liam groaned. "Listen, Stef -"

"Don't do it."

"I'm just not up for people today. Especially not those freaks."

"Liam." Stef paused for a moment, "usually your hermit-like tendencies are cute, but when you ditch me to tolerate our friends alone, I take issue."

Liam sat up whining. "Can't you blow them off?"

"After we missed their indoor barbecue last month, Frankie came by my place with a care package full of those designer freebies she gets. I felt so bad. I can't go through that again! I'd have to move and I can't afford to right now."

Liam sighed heavily.

"Please," she breathed. Liam felt his phone burning against his cheek.

"Fine," his exasperation rang out clearly. "Still got beer in your fridge?"

"Same place you left it." Liam shook his head at how pleased she sounded. "I'm heading over."

Liam didn't bother knocking. Letting himself in, he made a beeline for the fridge. He admired how well-stocked and tidy she kept it. He reached past the package of strawberries and pulled out two brown bottles. At some point he would have to learn how to deal with social situations without alcoholic assistance, but on that day he'd be forgiven. Liam kicked off his shoes before stepping into the carpeted living room. He pulled off some cushions from the sofa and threw them and himself onto the floor. That was how Stef found him half an hour later.

"You're absolutely right. I struggled to find a furnished apartment so that you could sit on the floor."

Not expecting a response, she sauntered past to her bedroom. Liam heard her shuffling about in her bedroom, likely changing out of her work clothes. Moments later he felt her climb onto the seat behind him. Peeking through a gap in his arms, Liam saw her legs curled beneath her, bare against the cushionless couch. His eyes followed the jagged scar on her left thigh. She definitely changed. Liam had only ever seen her wear shorts that small at home. Through the armhole of her oversized hoodie she held a can of cider. Liam sat up and leaned against her knees. He raked his hands through his hair one too many times.

"What's wrong?"

Liam let out a deep sigh and told her about his day, sparing no detail about the store.

"Lean forward," she said gently rubbing his neck. Her breathing got louder and more pronounced. Without realizing it, Liam fell into the rhythm she set. His shoulders slumped and he rested his head back onto her.

"Gonna have to find a new shop," he whinged.

"There's one just behind your place."

"It was easier to cross the street. The other one is two corners away." He knew he was whining and hated the pitch of his voice. "Actually," he cleared his throat, dropping a couple octaves, "it would make more sense to just move."

"Ha! You're in worse financial shape than me."

Liam's hands shot back into his hair. Stef leaned over and wrapped her arms around his shoulder.

"Hey," she rested a hand on his heart, "listen to me." She chastely kissed his cheek. "Odds are they didn't get a good enough look at you. You have very common features, no criminal record and an abysmal social media presence. It's not likely they'll come looking for you."

"I go to that shop a lot."

"Yeah, to pick up cereal. No one there knows your name or where you live. They probably know you as the man-child that can't feed himself properly."

Liam stroked her arm. He appreciated the comfort, backhanded as it was. Stef ran her fingers through his hair a couple times before leaning back on the couch.

"I'm thinking of going back to therapy. Maybe you should consider it too."

Liam glanced at her over his shoulder. "Oh yeah? Same guy as last time?"

She shrugged. "Don't think so. It might scare him to learn I'm still alive. He was so sure I was suicidal."

"You did go through a weird period back then."

"Perhaps. He just had a really literal interpretation of 'I'm thinking of killing myself.'"

Liam chuckled, "You think that's an ambiguous phrase?"

Stef rolled her eyes. "When I say I want to die, I don't necessarily mean ..."

"To shuffle off this mortal coil?"

"Umm, sure," she said tucking a stray tendril back into her bun. "I just mean that I don't want to be this version of myself anymore."

Liam turned his body to face her better, bracketing her body with his arms. "I didn't know you believed in reincarnation."

She smacked his arm making him laugh again.

'I'm not sure I do. I mean that I don't want to be bound by the restrictions of this particular life I'm living. These bills, these people, these heartaches." She crossed her arms. "Can't help feeling sometimes that being a couple hundred miles away or a couple inches off my hair will change everything."

"Is that why girls cut their hair?"

Stef extended a leg to knee him. Liam saw it coming and moved so she barely grazed his shoulder.

"I guess that didn't convince him."

36

"Not really," she sighed. "I only just managed to avoid getting committed."

"That was a strange period." Liam traced small circles on her calf. "Do you still get that way?"

"Once a month."

Leaning back, they opted to sip their drinks and scroll their phones in silence. They stayed that way a while until Stef let out a frustrated groan.

"I'm so sick of people posting these motivational pics. As if changing your life is just that easy."

"It is if you're rich."

"Or sponsored."

Liam saw her fingers hovered in place. She continued to look at the picture with a curiously resigned expression.

"Do you ever feel like we've fallen behind?"

Her dark brown eyes met his. She made no overt motion to agree, but it was there all the same. Liam turned back to her, resting his elbow on the space beside her.

"It's like my growth got stunted along the way, delaying who I'm meant to be."

"And who is that?" Her tone was flat.

"Someone who's got their shit together. How about you, professor?"

Stef looked away.

***

When they graduated, things seemed to just fall into place. As expected, Stef got an internship at a prestigious firm in the city to keep busy until starting law school. Meanwhile, Liam, dazzled by the prospect of a career in journalism, sent off mountains of resumes and writing samples that landed him an unpaid position in an area he didn't care about. But it was a foot in the door and he could make it work. This was adulthood, and if that meant spending nine hours sitting at a desk hoping someone would throw a juicy article his way before he had to head across town to pour drinks for another five hours all so that he could afford to live, so be it. He was young and wouldn't entertain the thought of leaving even if he was working himself to death. Until his mother did.

The afternoon Liam got the call from the hospital informing him of his mom's stroke, the phones in the office continued to ring in details of stock increases and insolvencies. The day of his mom's funeral, the paper went out without a hitch. A day later, when he returned to the office, he did nothing but book a flight to his mom's home country and, ever the supportive friend, Stef packed up her stuff to join him. Liam didn't protest when she offered. He knew she needed this as much as he did. She was months away from signing away her life and could use a proper adventure.

As much as he wanted to honor his mother, Liam hoped to find himself in the way naive writers do when looking for material. He figured that maybe the key to that was finding out what happened to his father. He dreaded winding up at a dead end but found himself at a fork in the road. Months of research turned up two possibilities. Either his father was lying in a mass grave somewhere or he made it out and made another family. Curiosity spared the cat, and he turned back. Liam decided he'd rather not know.

***

"How's the job search going?"

Liam pushed a throw pillow onto his face which only somewhat muffled his screams.

"That bad?"

"I'm faced with either complete silence or rejection from places I don't even remember applying to." His hair stood at odd angles from the constant commotion.

"Maybe it's time to consider a life of crime," Stef joked monotonously.

"Bank robbery?"

"Start smaller. Something with less chance of getting caught."

"Sounds like a win-win." He looked up flashing her a cheeky grin, "If we make it, yay! If not, free room and board."

Stef shrugged, "I don't think I'd fair well. I've got a very specific skincare regime and I doubt they'd let me bring all my products."

Liam laughed. "Wouldn't it be great if you could?"

"That would mean that prison is more lenient than TSA." Stef pursed her lips for a moment. "Would you really be willing to give up your freedom for a sense of stability?"

"At this point I might." Liam tossed the pillow on his lap. "Anything not to fill out another fucking application."

Stef laughed darkly. "Just think, if you walked in on those guys actually whacking a guy, you could get thrown into witness protection. Then you'd get to start over."

"Or," he grinned menacingly, "we could just frame them for something."

"I don't know. I feel like it would have to be something like murder to qualify and I draw the line at arson."

They collapsed into laughter again.

"Well," she said, patting his hand, "time to start getting ready."

Liam pleaded silently. The dark centers of his hazel eyes were wide. She faltered for a moment then hopped up.

"We're going," she declared storming out of the room. "And comb your hair," she shouted from the other room.

"I'm opening the wine." He figured if that didn't help change her mind, it would at least slow her down.

"Red, please."

Liam made no effort to hide his sulking. His complaining stopped short of a tantrum when Stef emerged from her room already dressed. A white sweater hugged her close, pulling away from her midriff to come up a little higher on her neck. Below, leather pants were tucked into a pair of combat boots. Liam appraised her slowly. It took so little for her to look like she made a great effort. He swallowed hard and resumed his bitching. Smiling, she pushed a bundle of clothes into his arms and ushered him away. He was grateful he didn't have to go home. She knew him too well. Stef didn't trust him to come back out if he went home, so she rifled through her closet for clothes he'd left over the year. His annoyance faded as the clothes warmed his chest. She must have pressed them.

In the bathroom, Liam ran his hand under the water and dampened his hair, following his fingers with one of her many combs. He emerged in a navy button down and dark jeans. She looked pleased with the result, which made him a little smug. Stef handed him a glass which he promptly chugged. One refill later and they were out the door.

CHAPTER 6

Encouraged by the drinks, Liam voiced his opposition to everything from the cold, clammy weather to their friends' choice of gentrified Asian cuisine. Shielded by the drinks, Stef merely laughed at all his grumbling. Liam didn't dislike his friends, but he was aware of how exhausting they were. Stumbling into the restaurant fifteen minutes late, the pair found Frankie and Kim finishing their first round.

Francesca must have been a descendant of King Midas. From the glow of her skin and the flecks in her eyes, she seemed shrouded in gold. Frankie, as she was called by friends, had an intensity that frightened Liam. Aside from their admiration of Stef, Liam didn't think they had much in common and went out of his way to avoid any one on one time with her.

Frankie rose gracefully, allowing her dress to sway sensually around her. The soft brown dress matched her skin perfectly. She looked like a woodland deity; at least that was how Stef chose to compliment her style as they got pulled into a tight hug. Liam nodded his agreement. Frankie kissed their cheeks in thanks. Her partner, Kim, gave them a curt nod from her seat, preferring to keep physical contact to a minimum. She was the exact opposite of her paramour in that way; and almost every other. Sitting comfortably in a gray cardigan, Kim pushed her short hair off her face and tucked into the plate a waiter just set down. Her delicate features stayed permanently set in a scowl. Five years on and she still hadn't warmed up to the group. Liam never learned if it was due to their incestuous history or the the fact that there was a history that didn't include her.

The remaining couple shuffled in a while later, making no apologies for their tardiness. Liam, already halfway through his second beer, paid no mind. It wasn't a mystery why Frankie kept Frank on her arm all through high school. Together, they were a ridiculously named but picture perfect couple until the end of high school when they both decided they'd rather sleep with other women. Ten years later, serial monogamist Frank and reformed free spirit Frankie both settled down with women named Kim, creating the creepy foursome he and Stef dubbed 'the twins'.

The newest Kim squeaked her greetings though a blinding smile. As Stef gingerly kissed her deeply dimpled cheeks, Liam stifled a laugh when he got pulled into a crushing hug. The seams on Frank's shirt screamed as he held onto Liam. In spite of being built like a pickup, Frank thought himself a luxury vehicle. Liam thought he could stand to get his brakes checked. Frank never learned the simple pleasure of doing nothing and benefited from it. He was put together in a way Liam never tried to be.

Before they could finish with the greeting portion of the evening, Frank launched into his latest news. He took them on a virtual tour of his new house, ignoring the clinking of Frankie's ring against her water glass. Liam and Stef snorted into their drinks, having no interest in competing in this pissing contest. Over his refreshed glass, Liam rolled his eyes at Stef who giggled, earning her the attention of the newest Kim.

"So you're a lawyer, right?"

"Nah," Stef shook her head, "that ship sailed."

The new Kim leaned forward. "Why is that?"

"Didn't have it in me," Stef shrugged.

Kim's eyes widened at her blunt honesty. "It is a tough career path," she said, clearing her throat.

Stef took a large swig. She usually had a smarmy reply at the tip of her tongue, but she was getting tired of having to justify her choices.

"You passed up good money," Frank said, shaking his head at her.

Stef tipped her glass in his direction. "I'm all about that vie Bohème."

"And what about our intrepid reporter?" Frankie turned their collective attention to Liam, who choked in response.

"I couldn't find a flying dude to interview."

Once their orders were placed, Frank leaned in to check on Liam. "How is the job hunt going?"

Liam didn't bother with words, instead relying on downing his drink to convey the state of things.

"Send me your resume. I'll pass it along to some people I know."

Genuine concern marred Frank's charming face. Liam lost count of how many times Frank explained his job to him. It is related to finance or technology, or both. Either way, it wasn't an area Liam had experience in, so he wasn't sure how Frank intended to help. He appreciated the offer all the same. Noting Liam's discomfort, Frank led the conversation away from him which Liam thanked him by zoning out. He tuned into the music that played a little too loud to fade into the background. His fist clenched repeatedly on the table, drawing Stef's attention.

"What's with you?"

"Do you hear this DJ?"

"I hear his shit selection of music."

"Not his unnecessary additions to them?" His forehead wrinkled. "He keeps hitting that button but he's pressing it offbeat."

Stef smiled brightly, casting off his funk.

"I'm just being pedantic."

She nodded and they tuned back into the discussion of the dismal weather.

"Time to put up the twinkling lights," the newer Kim giggled.

"It's barely November," the other Kim interjected.

"It's basically the holidays! It's totally okay to decorate by Thanksgiving."

"Speaking of which," Frank's booming voice cut in, "we're not gonna make it this year. We're heading to Colorado to spend it with this one's side." He pulled the tiny woman closer, eliciting another giggle and eye roll from the respective Kims.

"Yeah, I don't think we're up to hosting two events this year. We've got both our families coming in to spend some time before the wedding." Frankie laid a gentle hand over Stef's, "But you two are more than welcome to join."

Kim didn't voice her opinion. The fire in her eyes spoke loudly enough.

Frank turned to Stef and asked if she was going home for the holidays.

"Not bloody likely," she snorted.

Half the table tensed. Frankie shot him a glare that softened his tone. "Have you spoken to them recently?"

"No more than our biannual check in." Stef moved her hands onto her lap.

Not sensing to let it go, the newer Kim pushed on. "You don't talk to your parents?"

"Long story."

"They disowned her," Frankie whispered.

"They didn't disown me." Stef pulled her drink closer. "We're estranged."

"What's the difference?" Frank asked.

"I maintain an element of control with estrangement."

Liam placed a comforting hand on her thigh.

The newer Kim rested her elbows on the table. Her hands cradled her cherubic cheeks. "What happened?" Her eyes gleamed with curiosity. Even the other Kim seemed more attentive. Frankie waved her off.

"Stef and I briefly dated after college and her parents weren't cool with it. There was a massive blow out."

"There was more to it than that," Stef added quietly.

"But that did play a part."

"Yeah," Liam spat, "but it was more them taking the side of that dickhead who tried to force himself on her instead of defending their only daughter."

Having graduated a year earlier than expected, Stef's parents gave her some latitude when she remained abroad after her and Liam's trip. When she returned with a masters in law and an interest in continuing her studies, it became obvious that she would not be going into practice. Tensions simmered when she came out but were quickly brought to a boil when a family friend tangibly demonstrated his affection for her. Her complaints fell on deaf ears as his word, as an esteemed professor, was taken over hers and she subsequently found great difficulty in continuing her academic pursuits. It was the last straw for her parents who expressed their disappointment by cutting her off.

While the table exchanged uneasy glances, the newer Kim missed them entirely.

"Wait, you're gay? I thought you and Liam were a thing."

Stef stared intently at her drink, wishing it would magically refill. Liam looked around for their waiter.

"She's one of them undecided types," Frank joked.

"Bi?"

"There's still time for them," Frankie added hopefully.

"Oh," Kim said after an eternity. "It must be hard to coincide that with your beliefs. I've always been interested in theology so I read a lot on Hinduism and the importance of family."

She was faced with blank stares all around. Stef's eyes narrowed.

"You think I'm Hindu?"

Kim's eyes doubled. "Aren't you?"

Stef slowly shook her head. "Why would you assume I was?"

"Well… because," Kim looked around for help. Frank fiddled with a loose straw on his placemat. "Because you're vegetarian, a yoga instructor and - " She motioned generally in Stef's direction.

"And?"

"Well, you're Indian, right?"

Liam snorted into his glass. Stef shook her head.

"Oh… so what are you?"

TIP #4

BE OPEN TO NEW EXPERIENCES

"Be sure to learn when to duck and when to catch."

CHAPTER 7

Vince hated Chicago.

No amount of darkness could disguise the ugly. The flashing purple light made everyone look tired. It wasn't even that late yet. He missed the energy of New York. In comparison, this place was just pathetic.

Vince lost sight of Andy a little after they entered. He pushed himself through the crowd until he bumped into a gaggle of women. They didn't even look his way. Shallow cunts. Vince sneered when he saw they were dripping off Andy. He didn't get it. The guy was all jaw and no personality. The asshole didn't even make an attempt to introduce him. Some welcome.

Vince continued towards the bar. Leaning against it, he took to eyeing the crowd again. There had to be some potential in there somewhere. It looked like he finally caught a break when two short skirts sidled up to the bar, their wearers looked barely of age. *Should be easy*, he thought, smirking to himself. Vince moved in behind the one in pink, pressing himself against her.

"You look like you could use a drink," he offered in her ear. The girl brought her shoulder up to her ear. Vince could feel her squirm. She was being tugged away by her friend who kept shooting him dirty looks. Vince placed his arms on the bar, effectively trapping her with his body.

"We're fine, thanks," the friend spat.

"I wasn't talking to you."

He grabbed pink skirt's hip roughly. Plastered and malleable, she stood still. The other one leaned over his arm to talk to her friend. Vince cut across the cockblock by motioning to the bartender for more shots. That could shut her up.

"I'm not drinking."

Vince rolled his eyes at her. Why couldn't bitches like her just stay home? They only come out to ruin everyone's fun. He looked back down at pink skirt. She looked like she was up for some fun.

"So a Shirley Temple then?" The strobe lights died on his yellowing grin.

"A Sprite is fine," she shot back.

Vince gave a short nod to the bartender who stood by. He let go of pink skirt to grab the drinks. A small pill dropped from between his knuckles into the clear liquid and fizzed away with the carbonation. He led them to his table. Andy could take that one. They could bore each other.

Unsurprisingly, Andy wasn't alone. Vince found him deep in conversation with another man. That meant that the other guy was talking while Andy looked off broodingly. Vince set the drinks down loudly and ushered the girls into the booth. Andy looked them over unimpressed. The other guy seemed pleased with the development. Vince narrowed his eyes at Andy who, once again, made no motion to introduce them. The guy didn't need any prompting.

"You're Vince, right? From the Big Apple?" He laughed alone at his own joke. "Settle in, let's drink to welcome the New York fuck-up," he said, happily swiping one of Vince's drinks. Vince quickly downed a shot, gripping the small glass tightly. He stared blankly across the table. He could see Andy sit up. Vince hadn't seen any emotion on his face before, but he swore that Andy almost looked amused. A vein jutted out of his thick neck. News of his failed attempt at branching out reached the midwest.

A few months back, a hit on a pawn shop went a little off script. Vince didn't think it went too badly, all things considered. He made it out with $2000 in cash and only one of the other two ended up in the hospital. The fact that no one was arrested did not appease his father who demanded he pack a bag. He was outraged to be exiled to the boonies to live among rats who acted like his name meant nothing.

Meanwhile, the asshole who still hadn't provided a name continued laughing.

"Didn't they send you away for trying to knock over a gas station? That's small thinking for such a big guy."

Just his luck. One colleague was a mute and the other didn't know when to shut up. The guy got up, shooting another of Vince's drinks. He stumbled over and patted Vince on the back.

"Good think your daddy runs things back home, huh?" He guffawed, "You get off with a paid holiday."

Vince, never having been on the receiving end of his own personality, was overcome with want for silence but found himself content with the crack under his fist as it collided with the guy's jaw.

Andy led him out of the club before the bouncers could reach them. He looked in better spirits, which only made Vince hate him more. The tall man pulled something from his coat and quickly stepped forward. From ahead, Andy turned and offered Vince a flask which he accepted. Maybe he wasn't so bad. Andy unlocked his car and slid into the driver's seat. Vince took a few attempts to open the door before falling into the passenger's side. The door was barely shut when Andy took off. Vince wanted to stay geared up for round two but his fighting words were drowned out by the gentle purr of the engine. He mumbled something about waking him but never heard a response as he gave in to the weight of his eyelids.

CHAPTER 8

A ndy was almost giddy. His lips curved slightly upward and his fingers tapped rhythmically on the steering wheel. All those prayers he sent heavenward; God was bound to listen to one. And He had.

He slowed his car to a crawl, keeping the stumbling man ahead just out of his headlights. Andy cut the engine and watched as his legs gave out. The answer to Andy's prayers stood slumped against a chain-link fence. From where he sat, Andy could hear the angry mumbling and drunken yelling that sent the sparse pedestrians about at this hour running across the street. A few blinks later and the street was abandoned. Like divine intervention. With a little assistance from rohypnol.

Gently, he pulled up alongside Dominic with the passenger window rolled down. Andy leaned across the empty seat, catching a flash of fear followed by recognition. They hadn't left on the best of terms at the club and Andy wanted to rectify that.

"We should talk."

Dom grumbled something unintelligible as he climbed in. Andy breathed deeply to relax his face. His passenger slurred his tirade, oblivious to the snores coming from the backseat. Andy pulled the car into an alley next to an empty office space. He looked over and saw Dom barely holding onto consciousness. In the rearview mirror, Vince remained sprawled across the backseat. It was almost too easy.

Hours later across town, Andy felt fresh in his third outfit change of the day. He sat in the dark of the car for a moment. A dull ache brought his attention to his recently injured hand. Andy squeezed the bandage, welcoming the rush of pain. This was it. The end of his life.

The fingers of his non-injured hand punched in a series of numbers on the screen. Voicemail — perfect. He called on the memories of men in their final moments and parodied the desperation in their voices.

"It's me. I have to get out of town. Things got really bad." Andy breathed loudly. "I won't be able to use this number anymore but if I make it, meet me at the same place as last time by three."

He hung up, beaming. The engine roared to life. Andy took a moment, caressing the steering wheel. It was a great car. He'd miss it.

CHAPTER 9

Spilling out of a bar, Liam and Stef giggled like school kids.

"So what flavor human are you again?"

"I'm the spicy variety."

A couple paces ahead, Liam walked backwards to face her.

"Yeah, but are you sriracha spicy or jalapeño spicy?"

Stef stumbled as she failed to land a smack, making Liam laugh harder.

"I forget because you got those Bollywood eyes. So where does that ass come from?"

"My mom," she laughed.

Liam reached to help her leap over a puddle at the end of the crosswalk. Plastered as they were, they managed to succeed in their search for dessert. Liam was impressed that the perpetually-cold Stef could eat ice cream in these near freezing temperatures. He enjoyed the little dance she made when she tasted the first spoonful. She had a habit of turning the spoon upside down to lay the ice cream directly on her tongue. Stef returned the spoon to the cup and licked the remnants of cream from her lower lip. She looked up to find Liam watching her. Her gloved hands grasped the paper cup. His empty hands felt claustrophobic in his pockets. She raised an eyebrow quizzically, but neither made a move to continue walking. Liam could have sworn her brown eyes darkened a shade. A blue light reflected off her wide pupils. The street was washed in it.

Part of the sidewalk ahead was taped off. Police ushered off the crowd that began to gather. Liam noticed a policeman hunched against a wall to the far side of the alley. He grabbed Stef's hand and pulled her along. Hidden from view around the corner behind the tape, Liam could just about make out the conversation between two officers.

"You okay?"

"Yeah, just wasn't expecting that."

"There are all sorts of freaks in this city."

"You ever seen something like that?"

"A hanging? Once, but that was a suicide a while back."

"No! I mean his feet."

Liam heard a pathetic chuckle. "No, that's fucked up. Dude probably got some fifth degree burns on them."

Stef tugged at Liam's elbow to guide him away. The street was crawling with squad cars. The commotion should have been accompanied by a dizzying racket, but Liam stood eerily calm. He looked over at Stef, her wide eyes once again illuminated by the flashing lights. He stared at her a moment then placed his hand on the small of her back and led them away.

The remainder of the walk to her apartment was silent. Stef threw him furtive glances the whole way. His face remained stony. She pulled him into a tight hug when they reached her building.

"Are you sure you don't want to stay over?"

Liam dropped a lingering kiss on her cheek. She didn't press the issue. He watched as she entered the building then turned the corner to his apartment.

Lights from passing traffic and the street below seeped into his room. Liam watched them enter and fade on his ceiling. Lying perfectly still, he felt waves on his mattress. It was mostly due to the drink but those blue lights still dancedd in his head. For longer than he could say, Liam felt like he was adrift, doing all he could to keep from drowning. Another car passed, shedding a light over him. He turned onto his side and drifted off. He could finally see the shore.

TIP #5

BE THE CHANGE YOU WANT TO SEE

"If you're going to wait for what life sends your way, don't hold your breath."

CHAPTER 10

S tef rested her hand on the lock. He wasn't coming up. She knew that, but a small part of her hoped. Shaking off the feeling and her coat, which she abandoned by the door, Stef settled in. The boots came off next, haphazardly. One landed near the couch while the other toppled over where she stood. She stared at them. It wouldn't take much to bend over to pick them up and carry them into her room. Stef took a step back, swaying further than expected. The shoes could spend the night there. She carried on to her room, tugging on her sleeves all the way.

The bathroom switch had a slight delay, so she stood in front of the mirror by the time the light buzzed on. Stef eyed herself appreciatively in the mirror. Turning to see all angles, she concluded it was an outfit worth repeating before peeling off the tight sweater. The pins holding her mane back went next. Her curls fell wildly around her shoulders, grazing the rounded tops of her pushed up breasts. Smiling dreamily, she went into her bedroom. Stef reached for an old shirt before grabbing a loose tank top. Though disrobed, she wasn't ready to lose the sultry person in the mirror yet. Strutting back into the bathroom in her sleepwear, Stef gave herself a last once-over. She reached for the coconut oil and slathered it over her face. Looking back up with her makeup half melted off made her chortle. After multiple rinses, her fresh face stared back at her relieved. The woman reflected back at her was recognizable, but now a different person.

"Who are you meant to be?" Liam's question shot to the front of her mind. Making her way through her skincare routine, Stef pondered all the answers that floated through her head. All of these years later and she still hadn't narrowed that down. She enjoyed teaching yoga, but, on occasion, an intense guilt would envelop her. It was no wonder her parents were angry. All the money they put into private schools and fancy degrees that she wouldn't put to use. She couldn't talk to them about it. She'd been given all the tools she could ever need to succeed. Her parents reminded her of that more than they ever told her they loved her. Most people would kill for her toolbox and she just set them aside. She didn't see the point. Stef never figured out what she wanted to build.

The woman in the mirror was beginning to blur around the edges. With no more stimuli, her brain started to shut down. Stef held onto the door frame for a moment while the room settled itself. Her uncertain feet worked valiantly to get her into bed. The room was spinning and showed no signs of letting up. Stef tried to breathe through it. A dizzy brain was bad enough but an uneasy stomach was the worst. It was just the drinks. She was sure of it. The gnawing in her gut should be gone by morning.

Stef emerged from her room rolling her curly hair into her usual bun. The scalding shower she took washed away some of the guilt from over-drinking last night. She pulled water out of the fridge and, forsaking the two steps it would have taken to reach for a glass, she put her lips directly onto the pitcher. Satisfied, Stef wiped the driblets from the sides of her mouth.

While the coffee brewed, she started up her computer and loaded the newspaper. Her eyes skimmed the headlines, munching on loose granola. She stopped chewing when she came across news of a murder. A shudder shook her as she read the familiar details. It was just as Liam described. The article gave a vague description of the area the body was found. She struggled to swallow. They had been there last night. Stef closed the computer and poured out half a cup of coffee. Leaning against the counter, she took slow deliberate sips. Her stomach was in knots again. She raised the mug to her lips but no further. Stef poured the remaining dark liquid down the drain. Glancing at the time, Stef made a mental note to call Liam when he was more likely to be awake. She made quick work of the dishes in the sink and wrapped up her routine.

Stef pulled the wide hood over her head. It fell low over her brow so her eyes barely peaked out underneath. She kept her head down and moved quickly, artfully dodging the others in her path. The cold air whipped her face, cracking her lips. She loathed that bright blue jacket. Frankie gifted it to her a few years back to 'lighten her wardrobe'. She would have preferred something more inconspicuous, but there were limited options hanging in her closet.

Stef was shocked to find Liam bouncing around the reception desk for her and doubly so when he joined her class. Excitement and inexperience jostled his every movement. Curiosity was getting the better of her, but she tried to maintain a professional distance. It was no use. The second her students cleared out of the studio, Liam was behind her. His eyes shone as he pitched her the solution to both of their problems.

"Witness protection."

CHAPTER 11

For the first time in a long time, Liam didn't hit the snooze button. He was awake long before the alarm went off. Yesterday's events replayed in his head without pause. A run in with the mafia and stumbling onto a crime scene in one day should be too much for a person, but it seemed to be the kick in the pants he needed.

Liam sat diligently at the diner with his laptop and a steaming cup of coffee for company. A rejection letter sat in his inbox taunting him. The company's name didn't ring any bells. Considering how many websites and forums he used, Liam lost track of where he had sent his resume. The top of his browser listed tabs holding more applications to fill out. He was a modern day Goldilocks: overqualified for some, underqualified for others, and every so often he fit the bill just right. Thinking back on all the applications he had sent out, Liam couldn't see the use in trying for any of these either. He'd heard that no one was hiring, but he didn't think that it was literally possible for *no one* to be hiring. He pushed away the sad thought that maybe no one wanted to hire him.

Liam hovered the mouse over a list of required skills. With a little effort, he could argue that he possessed some of them and could pick up the rest, but it felt pathetic. When was he expected to have picked up all of these skills?

Dear hiring manager,

I'm already roughly five-eighths of the person you're looking for and I'm desperate enough to change for you. Please judge me accordingly.

With a sharp huff, he gave up. Every click that closed a tab gave him a rush. It felt good to turn the tables on them, even if they didn't know it. He stopped at the last window. His eyes ran down a list of a different sort.

The sirens last night sobered him a little but not enough to comprehend the pages he looked up. Liam looked through the article he had opened last night, which led to another, and a few more. Reading up on crime in Chicago led him down a rabbit hole. Just when he was ready to climb out, a blue word sent him down a new tunnel. He blamed Stef. Not really, but it was her idea. She always had the best ideas. He had to speak to her. Liam scooped all of his things into his bag and made quick work of the bill. He didn't bother to shoot her a text. He knew where she would be.

Liam bounced around the reception desk waiting for her to arrive. Her eyes widened when she saw him.

"I gotta talk to you."

Concern washed over her face. "Are you alright?"

"Yeah, never better." He waved off her worry. "We have to talk."

"Can it wait?" she asked, barely appeased. "I've got a class in five minutes."

"Ditch it, this is big."

She rolled her eyes. "Liam, unless this is an emergency, you're going to have to wait." She smiled maliciously. "Unless you want to join in."

"I'm way too wired for yoga."

She nodded. "That's why I'm suggesting it. What are you on?"

"Coffee. Lot's of it."

"How many have you had?"

"Dunno. Lost count around eight."

"Eight cups of coffee?" The horror on her face rang out in her voice.

"Nah, eight a.m. I've been at it for a while."

Stef rubbed her forehead. Her face relaxed at his reduced risk of cardiac arrest.

"Seriously, we'll talk later."

Liam threw his head back and whined. Stef placed her hands on his shoulders, like a mother calming her child. "If you're gonna stay you have to participate." She added with a smirk, "You won't be able to talk."

Liam scoffed. "I think I can do both," he said with undue confidence.

Liam followed Stef into the studio. He shrugged off his excess layers and tossed them in a corner. The class shuffled in, exchanging quiet greetings and unrolling their mats. Liam looked around, suddenly feeling out of place. Stef caught his eye and pointed to a door at the back of the room. He went to collect a mat and tried to find a space close to her at the front. Calm sounds came out of the speakers. In a breathy voice Stef greeted the class and began instructing.

"Start by reaching towards the sky, palms facing inward and hold this position. Breathe deeply into your stomach."

Liam kept his eyes trained on her. For a moment, they made eye contact and he winked. Stifling a smile, she looked away quickly, but not before he saw some color rise on her cheeks. Stef pointedly avoided looking his way and continued her demonstration. Liam tried to focus on the poses until he saw her stand and circle around the students. He tried to follow her movements which would have been easier if he were an owl. A warmth covered his back when she approached, adjusting his shaking arms.

"Why did you have so many?"

"Needed the WiFi," he said raggedly. "Had to cut it at my place."

"And down into child's pose. Try to rest your behind on your heels as you stretch your arms in front of you." She leaned over him, gently pushing his head to the mat, and whispered into his ear, "Still, you hit the sauce a little hard, don't you think?"

"I needed something to drown my sorrows since I can't afford to live." Trying to stay balanced, Liam gritted his teeth. "Which is how I got this great idea."

Stef walked away, ordering new poses. "Really focus on your breathing," she instructed circling back towards Liam.

"I'm focusing on not tearing my groin."

A chortle escaped her. Stef maintained her distance for the remainder of the class. Before everyone left the room at the end, Liam was at her side. He was newly invigorated in spite of his struggle. There, with her on her knees rolling up yoga mats, he popped the question.

"How would you like to solve all of your financial issues?"

Stef raised an eyebrow. "What are you selling?"

"I'm not selling anything. I was looking at our options earlier and found the solution: government funding."

He looked on proudly as he watched her return the stray mats to their cubby. Stef glanced over her shoulder to find him standing smugly behind her. His hands rested in his front pockets and his eyes dropped over her figure.

"Because I hadn't already checked that?" Stef laughed sarcastically. "I don't qualify," she said standing up. His amused expression never wavered. Once again, curiosity got the better of her. "What did you find?"

He reached for her. "Witness protection."

Liam was ordered to find seats while Stef got them drinks from the gym's cafe. She returned from the counter, pausing among the tables to watch Liam at the corner table. He pleaded silently for her to sit. She sighed and obliged. Taking a sip from one cup, she pushed the other to Liam. He smelled the annoyingly floral scent of chamomile. He looked up to object to the cup and its contents. Faced with the stony Stef, he figured it would be safer to wait for her to speak first. Her mouth opened only over the brim of her cup as she stared over it. Liam took a sip to have something to do. He pulled a face at the flowery taste. Stef lowered the cup but not her gaze. Liam tapped his finger against the table, occasionally looking up to meet her indecipherable face. He couldn't bear the silence any longer.

"Just think about it. It would fix everything."

She pursed her lips and he continued.

"You want to go back to university but have a couple obstacles between your lack of money and your ex-advisor blacklisting you."

Stef crossed her arms and looked away. Liam, noticing her discomfort, reached across the table. "And we both know my situation isn't great. I mean the job hunt is going terribly and my finances are steadily getting worse."

She laced her fingers with his but remained quiet.

"Just think about it, Stef. We both could use a do-over. This is the only way."

Finally, she sighed. "Hypothetically speaking, what's the plan?"

"Get thrown into witness protection."

Her eyes narrowed dangerously. "Details!"

Liam straightened in his seat, leaned in and smiled. "You remember that crime scene we passed yesterday?"

Stef nodded. Liam pumped his eyebrows and gestured vaguely with his hands. Stef silently motioned for him to continue. He shook his head annoyed that she was missing the obvious.

"We say we have information about that."

"So we just lie to the police about a potential mob hit and all our problems are solved?"

"Not with that attitude."

Stef pinched the bridge of her nose. "How do we know the cops aren't in on it?"

"Not all of them would be dirty."

"How do we know that we don't walk into the station with this bullshit story and pick a dirty one? You have to admit, with our luck, it could happen."

Liam paused for a moment. "Simple," he smirked, "we pick a cop with an Irish name."

"And that accomplishes what?" Her brow furrowed into her brain.

"We know the bad guys here are Serbian. An Irish cop would probably work for the Irish mob if he were dirty."

Her eyes widened in disbelief.

"Yeah, okay. That sounds racist," he had the decency to wince, "but it has better odds of being true.

Stef took a comforting sip of tea. "You act like I should just know that."

"Think like me. We've got to operate with one brain now. It's the only way a plan this stupid will work."

Stef rolled her eyes, but was relieved that he wasn't entirely delusional. Drops dotted the table when she set down her drink. "And what exactly do we say?"

He shrugged so violently it closed his eyes.

"We say what I heard at the store."

"That's not enough."

"What?" His brow creased, "Sure it is. It totally proved those guys did it."

"It's inadmissible in court," Stef said, shaking her head.

"How?"

"It's hearsay."

Liam tilted his head.

"That's an out of court statement offered in court to prove the truth of a matter." Stef sat up. "I always thought it was pointless but I get it now."

Liam remained puzzled.

"It's a rule that prevents people - like us - from repeating things they allegedly heard out of court inside of court, since there is no way to prove it."

He shrunk in his seat. "But it proves their MO."

"It's not enough."

"What if we say we saw them do it?" He asked, leaning forward.

"In the dark alley with no confirmation as to the time of death or even if the murder took place there?"

"Oh," Liam said, deflated. "Fuck." His hands dropped to his lap as he slouched in the chair. Stef watched him with soft eyes. She bit her lip as if to stop herself from speaking. Liam looked up through his unfairly long lashes and she swore under her breath.

"Let's assume that the dude was killed in the way you heard. We know he was tortured with burns then shot and then hanged, right?"

Liam nodded.

"Okay then. To be a viable witness you have to actually have seen something. Like the death and/or torture or, at the very least, you have to place them at the scene at or around the time of death."

"How do we figure out what time that happened?"

"Hard to say. It's unlikely that all of that," Stef cleared her throat, "unpleasantness happened in that alley. It's too public."

Liam edged towards the end of his seat. "And we walked past that alley on the way to the restaurant around eight. Don't think there was anything there."

"Yeah, there were a lot of people out at the time. Someone might have seen something."

"We only passed by again after getting ice cream around one, but by then the police were there."

"No," her nose wrinkled, "we passed it after leaving the bar at midnight."

"We didn't reach that alley though. We crossed the road when your cravings hit, so we turned back."

Stef rolled her eyes. He cocked his head. "Besides, I doubt the body was up then."

"Why is that?" She asked, taking a long sip of her lukewarm drink.

"Because a car was pulling out of the alley at the time."

Meeting each other's eyes, they froze at the implication.

"That could have been them," she whispered.

Liam only nodded.

"Did you see anyone?"

He shook his head. "You?" His voice strained.

"No, but I wasn't really paying attention."

Liam felt his face warm, recalling last night. She had linked her arms with his; the smell of her shampoo surrounded him when he buried her face in the crook of his shoulder. Her lips brushed against his neck as she laughed at some stupid joke he made. Liam pulled at the fabric around his knees.

"Do you think it was them?"

Stef's voice pulled him back to the present. Liam shrugged. "Like you said, the actual murder probably took place somewhere else. That's just where they dumped the body."

Stef arched an eyebrow at the smile that cracked Liam's face.

"It's perfect."

She glared at him. He grimaced in response. "It's not great that someone died," he stammered. "Well, not great. I meant it's not good." He sputtered for a moment. "I'm not happy that someone is dead and in no way do I condone torture and murder. However, we barely have to lie now!"

Stef's lips pouted to the side.

"Think about it. We 'saw' them dump the body."

"So we say we saw them hang a body? Won't they ask why we didn't call the police?"

"No," he said, eyes gleaming. "Because we didn't know what was happening until later. Which is technically true."

Stef rested her arms on the table. "Explain."

"Here's how I remember last night," he smirked. "We met friends for dinner and drinks. At midnight we were walking home when our path was blocked by a car parked in that alley. We heard some dude talking and I remembered that voice. Then I saw one of them was around the car and I freaked. So we turned back, got some ice cream to calm down, and waited for them to leave."

"Can you describe the two?" Her tone was interrogatory. He smiled. She was playing along.

"I didn't get a good look at the fat guy, but the tall one definitely."

Stef held her hands up. "But I don't know what they look like."

"One is a beefy guy with a squashed nose. He's the one that came from New York and I guess the actual murderer."

"Really," she snorted.

"Yeah, just imagine someone pressed his nose down and it never sprung back. And the other guy looks like the sort of dude you find attractive. You know, with the height and chiseled face, only scary. Like that actor you like. The one with the eyes."

Stef rolled her eyes but nodded. She knew who he meant.

"So we 'saw' one, but heard the other guy. That way if they ask how you're sure it was them, you can bring up the conversation you heard."

His frown pulled his eyebrows down. "I thought you said it was inadmissible."

"To prove that they did it. Here, you're using it to identify them. People would believe that you'd recognize that voice because you're unlikely to forget what you heard."

His mouth formed a silent oh. "So we saw the scary one and heard the big guy. Do we say we saw the body?"

"No, it would raise too many questions. 'How did you find the body? Did you actually see them hang it? How come they didn't see you?'" Her head bounced with each question.

"Okay, okay. So we nearly ran into them, freaked, hid out for a bit, then went home. We didn't connect the dots until we saw the news this morning."

Stef sighed deeply. "It still feels a little circumstantial, but at least we could place them at the scene with the details of the crime. I'd say, hypothetically speaking," she emphasized those words, "anyone with that story would be a pretty important witness."

"Yeah," he said looking out of the window. "Hypothetically."

CHAPTER 12

S tef left the gym late in the afternoon with a grumbling stomach. The sun was already low in the sky and the street lamps were a pathetic substitution. She fiddled with the wrapper of the sandwich she picked up on the way home. Her apartment building came into view, comforting her protesting tummy. At least there was one organ she'd be able to quiet.

Liam's proposition had been weighing on her mind all day, throwing her off balance. It was stupid. She expressed that much in person, but at the back of her mind, she couldn't help but see the merits. At this point it wasn't all that unreasonable to want a fresh start. With each step, she added to the list of pros and cons. Aside from the very real threat of jail time if discovered, the con side wasn't doing much to compete against the chance to start over. If they could convince the police of their story, the payoff would be great, but that was a big if to contend with. By the time she reached her building, Stef settled on trying to convince Liam to back off. She'd let him down gently and encourage him to pursue some other harebrained scheme. An exhausted sigh hitched in her throat when a uniformed officer waiting by the door flashed her badge.

The drive to the police station was a frosty one. The policewoman had barely spoken two words to her since ushering her into the car and, to make matters worse, the air-con was on full blast. Moisture from Stef's still-damp hair seeped into her t-shirt. She was seething. Not only was she about to get arrested, but now was doomed to start her life behind bars with a cold.

Her fingers itched to wrap themselves around Liam's throat. What the hell was he thinking? Stef's spine was as taut as a bowstring as she followed the officer into an interrogation room. The door closed with a snap. She felt the air being sucked out of the room. Taking a seat, Stef regretted declining the offer of water. She had nothing to fidget with and no one to talk to. Yet. Her eyes darted to the door. She dreaded to think who would come through it. She had no idea what questions they would ask, much less how she would respond. *For fuck's sake, Liam,* she thought, chewing on her thumbnail. He had gone to the police without her. Tears prickled her eyes. Did he plan on leaving her behind? She had assumed that she was included in the plan. Stef took a deep breath to drown a sob. Surely there was only one thing the police wanted to talk to her about. Liam had definitely spoken to them and they wanted to confirm his story. A part of her considered telling the truth and putting an end to it all. She was well aware that there would be legal repercussions if she did. Fear filled that tiny room. Stef avoided her reflection in the two way mirror. She kept her head down and focused on peeling her already chipped nail polish. To those unseen observers she looked the part of the terrified witness.

Stef's nails were nearly bare by the time two suited individuals walked in. She could barely make out their names over the sound of her heartbeat. They stiffly took their places before launching into their questioning, making her jump in her seat. It wasn't long before they inquired about the nature of her relationship with Liam.

Her eyebrows shot up. "Could you be more specific?" She asked more spitefully than intended. One of the detectives scowled in response. Stef inhaled audibly.

"We're friends."

They looked unamused by her vagueness.

"Do you see each other often?"

"Define often." She wasn't sure how she would play this. The less she said, the better, but every word out of her mouth came out hostile.

The other detective spoke up. "When was the last time you saw him?"

"A couple hours ago at the gym."

"And before that?"

"Last night," Stef shifted in her seat. "We met some friends for dinner and drinks."

"Sounds often to me." The first detective rested his arms on the table. The large button on his sleeve scratched along the table as he moved. She raised an eyebrow.

"We're close I guess."

"You guess?"

Stef managed to bite back her reply but her face didn't get the memo. She went back to chewing on her nails.

"Can you tell us what you got up to last night?"

She stilled in her seat. Between the ride over and getting stared down by the detectives, all of her nerves were shot. Stef couldn't remember a time she'd felt so uncomfortable. She mustered any stray courage and described the evening in question. The tension between her shoulders eased as she got into her story. That was until the moment they mentioned a photo lineup. A binder was pushed towards Stef. Scrunching her face, she tried to remember Liam's descriptions of the men he saw. With a deep breath she flipped through the photographs, fighting off a smirk when she came across the mugshot of a man was a squashed face. It was a guess, but given this selection of photos, she felt confident that was the first guy. Her stomach dropped when they turned the page over. Cold eyes stared up at her leaving her deeply unsettled. The man they belonged to was attractive, just as Liam described, but something was just off about him. She didn't care to look any longer to figure it out. Stef took solace that he was stuck in 2D instead of in the room with her. She was less sure of her decisions, but she pointed to him regardless. Stef didn't look up to see if they bought her story. The way her hand shook might have sold her.

"Someone will guide you out shortly."

Their demeanor softened. Once again she was in the room with nothing to do but wrap her arms around herself.

The room she was brought to was empty save for a man in the corner. He sat with his head in his hands. The dark mop of hands sent a ripple along her skin. She walked up to him, hands on her hips, and waited. Liam looked up sheepishly.

"What did you do?"

No amount of whispering disguised the venom in her voice.

"Take a seat."

"Liam!"

He threw his hands up in surrender. "I'll talk. Just sit down first."

Stef threw herself into the chair beside him. Her large brown eyes overflowed with the tears she had been holding back.

"How could you actually do this?" *Without me* silently punctuated her question.

Stuck in that waiting room for hours, Liam had plenty of time to reflect on his idiotic decision. He told her the same thing he'd been repeating to himself.

"They are bad guys."

She said nothing.

"It was definitely them."

"You don't know that."

"Well," he shrugged, "the officers outside think I do."

"And why would they think that?" The sarcasm that dripped freely from her tongue went ignored.

"Because I told them so."

The urge to strangle him resurfaced. Stef clenched her fists in her lap. Try as she might to remember, the speech she had rehearsed to convince him out of this plan vacated her mind. She focused instead on their current predicament. Best case scenario, their story would become key witnesses in a criminal case against the local Serbian mob. Worst case, they would get sued for defamation and charged with obstruction of justice. The more optimistic voice in her head reminded her that it would only be slander if it wasn't true; so that might be one less charge against them. If it were, in fact, true, then two bad men would be off the streets.

Stef folded her arms over the back of the chair and buried her head in her sleeves.

"How could you come without me?"

Liam placed the softest kiss on her temple.

"I wasn't going to leave you," he whispered into her hair. He ran a hand down her thick braid. "I told them about you immediately. I just thought it would be safer if fewer people saw you."

He pulled her closer as she began to sob. Stef faced him, feeling every inch of the distance between them.

"This is bad."

INTERLUDE

BE ADVISED

Sometimes shit is going to hit the fan. Accept it and move on.

CHAPTER 13

This city was a pain in the neck. Literally.

Vince woke with stiff shoulders and a splitting headache. Independent from his hangover, he felt wrong. The whole city was wrong. The pizza was too thick, the hot dogs had too much on them and it was fucking cold. New York was cold, but this made him envy the dead. His views on the great city would be forever tainted by the circumstances that made him leave his home. He was exiled. They claimed it was for his own good. He felt like it was a slap to the face. "Lie low," they said. He grumbled at being hidden away like a pregnant teen. It was worsened by the collective here coming straight from the old country. He was a New Yorker and here these midwestern hick immigrants were speaking in tongues.

There is nothing like a hangover to kick off a new life. He spent the better part of the day before passed out or puking up his guts. Fucking Andy. It was his fault and he didn't even have the decency to answer his phone. Vince might have insisted that Andy take him out, but he didn't have many options. The kid was still too young to be any fun and since the tall fucker wasn't much of a conversationalist, Vince turned to the drinks. He wasn't sure if he'd had too many or if they were brewed stronger out here, but either way Vince woke to a jackhammer in his head. Though the grogginess and bruised knuckles were physical reminders of two nights ago, they came unaccompanied by any memories.

The call of nature was turning urgent. Vince groaned at the thought of leaving the warmth of the bed. It worsened his already foul mood. Angrily he threw off the sheets which landed halfway off the bed. His feet made

73

contact with the glacial floor, eliciting a barrage of curses the whole way to the toilet. In the midst of the ringing between his ears, Vince could just about make out knocking at the door. An impatient voice called out something he didn't understand. It was likely an unwelcome neighbor. The building was filled with foreigners with their weird cuisines that blended together in the halls, doing nothing for his nausea. The knocking persisted. Vince charged out of the bathroom without stopping at the sink for a quick rinse.

"Keep your panties on, asshole."

Vince unlocked the door, continuing his tirade against the knocker.

"The fuck you want?"

He swung the door open to find a large black man standing smartly in the hall. "Vincent Petrović?"

"Who the fuck are you?"

"Chicago PD. We have a warrant."

TIP #6

PACE YOURSELF

"Slow and steady gets the cheese."

CHAPTER 14

Charlotte Moreau circled the caffeine dispenser like a vulture. She waited for the predators to clear out so she could claim the remains of their brew. There was barely enough to reach a quarter of a cup. Accepting that the quality of this stuff wouldn't pass muster as an espresso, she reached for the coffee grounds, filled the machine and waited. With a quick glance behind her, Charlotte pressed the little button that poured out the beautiful dark liquid with a frothy finish. She raised the cup to her lips and hummed in approval as she began the walk back to her desk. The one piece of advice she took from her sisters was to keep her talent for making excellent coffee tightly under wraps. Not that it mattered much, with the state of the art machinery the taxpayers blessed them with for just that. Standing at a respectable 5'3, Charlotte was an unusual fit at the Federal Bureau of Investigation. Something about her height, round face, and bobbed blonde hair went against the expected picture of a federal agent. A lifetime of fighting to be seen left her overly concerned with being taken seriously. On her first day, she introduced herself as Charlie, fully aware that no one in all her thirty-one years had ever called her that.

Charlie wiped at the spot where a stray droplet of coffee found her white shirt. Content that a stain would not form, she took a moment to appreciate the sight before her. Papers scattered across her desk. For a moment, she wished that her caseload reflected her parents' perception of what her job entailed.

"Oh honey, I'm sorry."

Her mother dropped her gaze, choosing to focus on clearing the table. It was not the reaction Charlie expected.

"What for?"

Her father placed a comforting hand on her shoulder.

"Don't worry, champ." He pulled her into a tight side hug. "Take this time to show them what you're made of. Give them time and they'll see how capable you really are."

"What are you guys talking about?"

They exchanged knowing glances between themselves, regarding her with unmistakable pity. Any reaction would have been preferable to this patronizing tone. No reaction would have been better.

"I wanted this transfer."

The silence was palpable. Her mother played with her hair gingerly.

"Really?" She asked as though daring Charlie to lie.

Her father seemed incredulous. "Is organized crime even really still a thing?"

A knock on the gray divider brought her back to reality. A colleague motioned in the direction of the conference room. Charlie scrambled to grab her tablet while swallowing several large gulps of the still hot coffee. She coughed and sadly left her mug half full, knowing it would be cold and congealing by the time she returned.

Charlie took her place among the audible swallowers and heavy breathers. Her supervisor, Sam Greene, barely got out a greeting before someone's phone went off. Charlie shot a look in the offender's direction. It went unnoticed as everyone was immersed in collectively scoring through the files that entered their inboxes. Sam commenced the debrief in a soothing monotone.

"A man was found hanging in an alley in Chicago two nights ago. The victim's name is Dominic Ilić. He was a member of the Serbian mob and, as it turns out, a police informant."

Charlie raised her eyebrows in agreement with the murmurs around the room. Sam continued unfazed.

"Cause of death was a gunshot to the head, but he showed signs of torture consistent with a series of murders committed here with the suspected involvement of the Petrović family."

Sam's square face remained neutral. His rough features masked the soft eyes that briefly made contact with Charlie, who hid a pleased smile as she looked back down to the file.

"Vincent Petrović just so happens to have moved out there earlier this week. He's got a rap sheet in New York with multiple counts of assault - both simple and sexual - drunken disorderly, and an attempted burglary. He was arrested this morning; we fly out in two hours."

Charlie fixated on the file in front of her, noting the time of arrest. Eight fifteen. The clock on the wall showed it was just after ten. She scrunched her face. Minimal as it was, Charlie hated cases in different time zones. It made her feel like she was playing catch up.

There are those for whom success looks effortless. Charlie wasn't one of them. The energy she put in to just keep up was a workout in itself. As the youngest of three daughters, Charlie calculated that she spent the better part of her life catching up. She failed in the height department and her sisters, having a good five years on her, made competing academically impossible. They were well settled into their careers and families by the time Charlie got accepted into the bureau. Though she couldn't brag about her work, she found her badge to be a useful tool to shut them up about her stunted social life. She mentally kicked herself for hoping that she'd have a chance to stand out in such a small team joining the Chicago branch. What kind of person tries to take advantage of a man's death to get ahead?

Arriving in Chicago, the small team went straight to the local FBI building. They barely stepped foot into the office when a deep voice called out from beside them.

"SSA Greene?"

The voice belonged to a medium sized, dark haired man near the doorway. They must have passed him on the way in. He stood unnaturally still; Charlie could see why they hadn't noticed him.

"Field Agent James Horne," he said reaching out his hand, startling the shirt that lay crisply against his body. Horne firmly shook Sam's hand and pointed towards the door, never giving Charlie a second glance.

"Just got a call from the medical examiner. Been waiting for you." His thin lips did a terrible job of holding back his impatience.

"Let us set our bags down then you can lead the way." Horne bristled at Sam's tone. Charlie smirked as they were guided to their temporary office space. On their return, James set a brusque pace for the visiting agents. Sam marched elegantly down the long fluorescent lit hallway and out of the building. Charlie kept up as calmly as her short legs would allow.

The group was greeted by a familiar, sterile smell. The medical examiner, a curvy bespectacled woman, emerged from the back of the cold room with a slight waddle, suggestive of pregnancy. All three had the good sense not to mention it. Taking a step back, Horne deferred to Sam who started the questioning.

"What can you tell us about the victim?"

The medical examiner moved around her desk and grabbed a folder from the top of the pile. She ushered the agents over to the fridge holding the body. Sam winced at the state of the victim, who lay coldly on the slab draped in a white sheet. "The bruising on the face and abdominal region are consistent with moderate blunt force trauma. The coloration and minimal swelling tells us it happened hours before death."

"The police report states the victim was in a brawl earlier in the evening," Charlie interjected. "Did that contribute to the cause of death?"

"No, he died from a single gunshot wound to the head. Nine millimeter. The downward angle of entry means he was likely sitting or kneeling. The recovered bullet was sent off to ballistics, but the police weren't hopeful when I retrieved it."

Sam creased his brow. "Unregistered?"

"Exactly." The medical examiner looked up, finally taking stock of the agents. She eyed Sam appreciatively before giving Charlie a knowing beam. Charlie returned it, looking down at the lanyard around her neck. She couldn't make out the last name, but the first was clearly visible. Rosalia.

"Just like in New York," Sam's face hardened. "What can you tell me about the burns?"

Rosalia scrunched her nose. "They are extensive, to say the least. Localized exclusively to the feet. There was no blistering, as expected with a slow burn. I'd describe it more as 'exploded.'"

Rosalia lifted the sheet to show the victim's feet. Horne whistled from somewhere behind them.

"Was he still alive when it happened?" Charlie asked, leaning in for a closer look.

Rosalia shrugged. "It's hard to say. There are no signs of healing, so it happened either immediately prior to or very shortly after death."

"How shortly after?" Charlie tilted her head.

"Likely in a matter of minutes."

"What about the hanging?" Sam thumbed through the folder Rosalia set down beside the body.

"That was definitely postmortem," she replied a little too cheerfully. "There was no bruising on the neck, so he was strung up after he was shot."

Charlie moved around to the victim's head, paying attention to his neck. The overkill matched the New York crimes, but there was something she couldn't put her finger on.

"Have you determined a time of death?" Horne chimed in, folding the sheet back over the victim's feet.

"The temperature last night makes it hard to calculate precisely, but best guess it between ten thirty and eleven last night."

"That fits the timeline," he added curtly. The medical examiner looked to Horne, expecting him to continue; instead, his focus went to his watch. Charlie noted that he would be pleasant to look at if not for the perpetual annoyance that graced his face.

"Oh," Rosalia sighed questioningly.

"The body was discovered around one fifteen in the morning. The Triple Crown was closing up and a bartender taking out the trash found him." He recited nearly verbatim from the report. "A witness saw the perps at eleven p.m. in the alley. He was with his girl at the time. She was called in yesterday afternoon to give her version of events."

Charlie was eager to watch those interviews. She craved new information only slightly more than she wanted to leave that cold room.

CHAPTER 15

On the screen, a young male looked calmly between the officers in front of him. The camera rested to the left of them both, granting an unobstructed view of the witness.

"Liam Broci?"

"Yes," he said, reaching up to remove his beanie. Dark waves grazed his neck while the rest stayed pressed down where the hat had been. He seemed strangely calm, given the circumstances. Charlie observed a slight movement on his left arm, a shaking as though his hand was moving underneath the table.

"You mentioned having some information about the murder that took place last night."

"Yeah, yeah I think I might know who did it." He spoke clearly, if not a little quickly.

"Go on."

Liam launched into a description of the night before and the conversation he overheard in the shop, enthusiastically providing details of the alleged perpetrators. He seemed at ease with the detectives' questions. His face soured when presented with the photo line up. Looking over the photos, Liam's lips tensed for a moment so quick, Charlie thought she had imagined it. She turned to Sam who quirked an eyebrow, acknowledging the flash of emotion. Genuine fear painted Liam's face as he pointed to Vincent Petrović and Andrija Durić. Just past Sam, Charlie could make out Horne's glare. His jaw clenched but, thinking nothing of it, she returned her attention to the screen. The others seemed content to move on, but Charlie tried to stop them. She asked them to rewind the tape a few seconds but no one paid her any mind. They brought up the next tape. She remained focused on Liam's minimized face. It might have been a nervous tick, but just before they stopped the video, Charlie could have sworn she caught a flicker of a smirk.

The monitor filled with the image of a young woman whose eyes darted around the room the second the video began to play. Loose tendrils around her face dripped onto her shirt soaking her shoulders. Black flecks littered the table as she picked at her nail polish.

"Stefanie Moreno?"

The detectives startled her when they commenced their interrogation. She nodded. She continued to look between them and the door.

"Do you know why we've asked you to come in today?"

She nodded again, this time bringing her index finger to her mouth. She chewed on the nail, keeping her eyes firmly on the table. When asked about the nature of her relationship with the other witness, the woman crossed her arms. Her tone became clipped and defensive. Charlie tilted her head at the change. Stef tensed again when asked to describe the events of that night. Nervously, she took them through the sequence of events.

"Around midnight I was ready to go home," she said, picking again at the remaining polish on her thumb. *"We were having a good time just joking around then Liam stopped. He got so pale."* She laced her fingers on the table. *"I had to pull him away. We went back the way we came and hid in a McDonalds until he calmed down. It wasn't until I read the news this morning did I put two and two together."*

Her eyes widened when asked to pick out the men in the alley. Barely audible, she confessed that she hadn't gotten a good look at them in the dark. A detective set out a series of photographs regardless. She took her time looking at the faces. After a couple of beats, she shakily pointed to two of them, hesitating a moment with Andrija's picture. Charlie tried to ignore the collective murmurs of confirmation around her. How could they be so sure when the witness wasn't?

That was that. The stories matched. The timeline fit. Everyone around her seemed content. Cut and dry, they said. Charlie bit her lip. It seemed way too easy.

CHAPTER 16

Off an exit, just outside the city limits, Andy contently stirred a small cup of something that passed for coffee. Dominic was dead. Vince was probably getting arrested. It was a little last minute in terms of an escape plan, but it came together beautifully. A few more minutes and all loose ends would be tied into a pretty bow. He was so close to a new life.

Andy watched a blue sedan pull into the parking lot. He fixed worry onto his handsome face. Careful not to let any amusement come through, he watched James Horne breathe a sigh of relief upon spotting him. Andy tightly grasped the cup in his hands, refusing to look up as James settled in across from him.

"I got your message."

Andy ignored James' attempt at conversation. In order to sell this, he needed to properly bait him. He counted the ripples in his cup, letting James stew in the silence.

"We found Dominic not long after you called. A warrant is being issued for Vince."

Andy took a long sip hiding a pleased grin.

"What can you tell me about last night?"

Dramatically exhaling, Andy recounted his twisted version of his day with Vince. He made a show of darting glances around the room and out of the wide windows.

"At the club Dom started getting in Vince's face. Didn't take long for Vince to deck him."

"Do you know what Dom said to him?"

Andy shook his head. "Didn't speak to him at all." Their short discussion about Mischa was irrelevant to the current narrative. "Anyway, we got thrown out and Vince started yelling about finishing what he started. I thought he just wanted to teach Dom a lesson. He tells me to bring up a toolbox to what I thought was his apartment. Next thing I know, he comes in with a body over his shoulder. It's Dom."

James ran a hand over his gelled hair. "Did you see what happened next?"

"The guy turns on a blowtorch. After the story he told earlier I didn't want to stick around."

"Wait," James said with narrowed eyes. "You said you were in an apartment you thought was his. How did you get there?"

Andy swallowed hard. "Vince drove us from the club. He parked in some alley and threw the keys and the box at me." He rested on his elbows. "Listen, it happened so fast. One minute we're having a few drinks, the next, the guy goes full Reservoir Dogs."

James whistled low before assuring him that he was safe. Andy felt his lip twitch, so went back for another sip. James asked him to come in to relay the story to his team. Andy widened his eyes with feigned fear.

"No, it's okay. Your story confirms what we were told earlier. It also explains your presence there."

Andy's stomach dropped as though he missed a stair.

"Someone saw me?"

"Yeah. Leaving the scene. Someone came in and told us pretty much the same thing you did."

"Oh, really?" His mouth was set in a hard line. Andy downed his drink, trying not to choke on the anger that tightened his throat. He underestimated their investigative abilities which is why he didn't leave breadcrumbs so much as neon arrows pointing to Vince.

"They got people looking for you. My boss will be thrilled we got to you first."

Andy's eyes sparked with suspicion. "You tell anyone you were meeting me?"

"No, of course not." James went on about the protection they would provide him. Andy nodded along and agreed to follow along shortly. With a firm handshake, James went on his way, leaving a fuming zombie in his wake. All that trouble to get a new life and it got stolen from under his nose.

The Lord giveth and the Lord pulleth the rug from under thee.

TIP #7

CHOOSE YOUR CONFIDANTS CAREFULLY

"The thing about sticking your neck out for someone is you can't see who is wielding the ax."

CHAPTER 17

Was the economy so bad that the police couldn't afford to turn on a *fucking heater?* Vince wasn't one to think about unimportant things like the economy until he could directly feel the effects, but thinking about funding and politics distracted him from his current reality. Limited knowledge on the matters meant he wasn't distracted for very long. He spent all morning in a cell with no offer of anything. The pigs were treating him like a common criminal.

Murder. These assholes were accusing him of murder. That's what they said when they dragged him out of his apartment. That and assaulting an officer. "Land of the free," he scoffed. Apparently you can't protect your freedom in your own home when the police decide to barge in with bogus charges. They had nothing on him. They were just trying to intimidate him. Vince sat up in his chair. They probably just got word that he just arrived and were making a big deal of showing they knew all about him. They didn't, but they were gonna.

The door hung open, revealing a pretty little thing. Vince puffed out his chest. Clearly this wasn't serious, otherwise they wouldn't have sent preteen Barbie in. He ran his eyes slowly over her form. She probably had nice tits, if only she didn't hide them in a man's shirt. Petite frame. Not bad, just too serious for his liking. She parked her pert ass across from him. He could see his face over her shoulder in the mirror.

"Vincent Petrović?" Her voice was deeper than he expected. He nodded once.

"My name is Charlotte Moreau, from the FBI." His eyebrows shot up. He definitely wasn't expecting that. His lips tightened. What did the FBI want with him? How was she working for them?

"What happened there?" She motioned towards his bruised knuckles. Vince moved his hands to his lap.

"Nothing for you to worry about, darling."

She stared at him plainly.

"Eventful week, huh?" Her tone was sweet and even. Something about it reminded him of how his mother spoke, as though she already knew what he would say. He hated that.

"What can you tell me about Dominic Ilić?"

Vince shrugged. "Don't know him."

"You worked together."

His nostrils flared. "It's a big company."

"So I've gathered."

He could smack that look off her face. His fingers flexed under the table.

"You were at the same club two nights ago."

"Me and lots of people."

"You were seen fighting him."

Her lips turned upward. Vince scowled pushing back in his chair.

"Is that where you got those bruises?"

Vince folded his arms over his chest, tucking his hands in at his sides. He looked around for someone else to talk to.

"Where did you go after you got thrown out?"

If his face scrunched any further it would cave in on itself. Charlotte moved around some papers on the table in front of her. "I mean, obviously you left alone." A hint of a smile graced her face. "Can't have been very impressive for the girls at your table to watch you lose a fight to Dominic. Wasn't he like half your size?" She looked him over. Vince pulled his jacket closed. He was increasingly unimpressed with this woman.

"Did your friends at least come out to get you?"

"Listen here, bitch," Vince shot forward only to stop when the door creaked open. A tiny balding man flew in, his oversized jacket flapping around him.

"Keep quiet."

The man loudly set his things down and noisily dragged a chair around the table to sit beside Vince, who watched him angrily.

"Who the fuck are you?" He roared.

Charlotte rested her chin on her palm and waited for them to settle.

"I'm your attorney," the small man replied matter-of-factly, continuing to rummage in his briefcase.

"Mr. Petrović never asked for one."

The lawyer continued scavenging, his head nearly inside the case.

"Nevertheless, his employer sent me."

He emerged from the leather bag with a pen in hand. He nodded at Vince who rolled his eyes in response. The lawyer looked across the table to Charlotte whose eyes glimmered with mischief despite her impassive face. Vince narrowed his eyes again at her.

"Tell me about Andrija Durić."

Vince could see his lawyer scribbling at his elbow but said nothing. He followed suit.

"Are you two close?"

He didn't like the way she asked that. Not that it was any of her business, but why ask about that prissy bastard? She was probably just another bitch that creamed herself at the thought of him.

"I know you work together too, but are you a little more?"

Vince slammed his meaty hand on the table. She didn't even jump.

"The fuck is that supposed to mean?"

The lawyer shushed him. He saw the corners of her lips quirk, riling him further. Charlotte kept her eyes trained on Vince as she set out a series of photos neatly before him. The lawyer brushed against him slightly when he leaned in for a better look. Vince continued to stare down Charlotte. He didn't want to give her the chance to surprise him. She was up to something; he could read her like a children's book.

"Do those look familiar?"

Vince held her gaze for a beat then looked down. He continued to say nothing.

"What are we supposed to be looking at?" The lawyer asked on his behalf.

"Crime scenes." Charlotte rested her arms flat on the table. She motioned to the selection to his right. "These happened in New York. Your client was a named suspect for them."

Vince gave the pictures a cursory glance before looking back at Charlotte.

"He was never charged for any of these; also, they are out of that jurisdiction, so if you have a point I suggest you make it."

Charlotte reached over to the pictures closest to Vince. He scoffed at the lack of ring on her hand. Figures.

"These were taken two nights ago. Recognize anyone?"

The row of pictures in front of him showed a body hanging in an alleyway, just like the surrounding photos. The next picture over was of the same body, now laid on the ground with a visible face. It was the dickhead from the club. He looked back up at her, her face now hardened to an unreadable expression. Teachers always said his literary skills left much to be desired.

Charlotte sat back in her chair. "Notice the similarities? This MO was completely foreign to Chicago until two nights ago. Much like your client."

"Do you have anything more concrete or are you building your case on coincidence?"

An eyebrow arched high on her head. "Coincidence? Your client comes into town, has a public altercation with the victim who later turns up dead in the exact fashion your client was suspected of using back home."

Vince cleared his throat. "I know nothing about it," he pushed the photos back to her. "Any of it."

Charlotte gently fingered the pictures back into place.

"Strange. Seeing as someone matching your description was seen at the dump site."

Vince crossed his arms again, his fists clenching at his sides.

"Can you tell me about Thursday night?"

He let out a huff that would shock a bull.

"You're not doing yourself any favors," Charlotte continued. "This could all be cleared up if you just tell us what happened on Thursday night."

Vince mumbled something under his breath.

"What was that?"

"I don't remember," he roared before the lawyer could stop him.

"Interesting."

"I got a little drunk and spent all of yesterday in bed. I didn't kill anyone."

Charlotte's nose wrinkled. "Your defense to having been seen at the dump site is that you were drunk and don't remember?" She stared him down. "Where is Andy?"

Vince had no time to hide his reaction.

"How the fuck should I know?"

"Why are you protecting him?"

"I'm not," his voice tore through the small room. The lawyer patted his arm which Vince quickly ripped away from him. "I don't give a shit about that pretentious fuck."

"Clearly he feels the same about you if he's letting you take the fall for this."

Vince's eyes shot open. That smug look was back on her face.

"He was seen with you at the dump site."

TIP #8

BE ASSERTIVE

"If you have a voice, speak up. If you don't, write in bold."

CHAPTER 18

L iam's interview was queued up for the fifth time that afternoon. After seeing Vince back to his cell, Charlie felt weighed down. Something was off. Vince was an ass, that much was obvious. Although all signs pointed to him, her gut told her otherwise. Charlie reviewed Liam's file as the introductions started playing.

Sometime after the third viewing, she started referring to him as 'kid' even though his ID showed him to be twenty-six. Charlie requested to lead the follow up interview with him. Her heart sank when informed he had already been moved into protective custody while awaiting placement in WitSec. She consoled herself by replaying his interview. As he started to speak, she pressed the earbuds deeper into her ears. To call it coincidence was a cop out. Charlie was looking for another way to explain how Liam just happened to stumble onto the scene of the very crime he'd heard described earlier. *Though*, she thought shrugging, *after meeting Vincent, it was possible.* Sure, he would never be accused of having forethought or common sense, but even he must know not to plan a murder in public.

Charlie stood up quickly, earning some curious stares from the people around her. She pushed in her chair as inconspicuously as possible and scanned the room for Sam. He hunched over his laptop at a borrowed desk in the corner. Stretching slightly, Charlie threw on her jacket and strutted in his direction.

"What can I do for you?" Sam didn't look up. There was a roughness to his voice that suggested he hadn't spoken in a while. The stronger part of her brain reminded her that she hadn't spoken and needn't apologize; the word slipped out all the same. Sam lifted his green eyes, that seemed unbothered by the interruption. Charlie cleared her throat.

"Do you have a minute?"

Sam set down his pen and leaned forward on the desk. It creaked as it slid against the linoleum floor. There was a moment's hesitation in her brain that her mouth didn't register.

"Something's off about this case."

Two deep lines appeared between his eyebrows. He nodded for her to continue. The reasonable part of her brain begged her to take a minute to wait for the right words. Again, her mouth was thrilled at the prospect of an audience.

"I think we have the wrong guy."

Sam looked around the room. Charlie tensed. She hadn't meant to be so brash.

"Let's get some fresh air."

Sam led Charlie to a small cafe just down the block. They said nothing as they stood in line. Charlie avoided looking his way by scanning the board of overpriced drinks. All the while, the warmth seeping through the left side of her jacket made it impossible to ignore Sam's hulking frame. When their turn came, she ordered an americano while he opted for a hazelnut latte. He pushed her towards the tables while he paid. They stuck to small talk until their drinks were dropped off. Charlie picked hers up immediately while Sam turned the mug on the table. The cup stilled in his hands.

"What's on your mind?"

Charlie winced at her scalded tongue. She'd have to deal with that feeling on top of everything else.

"I have some serious doubts."

The heat from his cup must have gotten too much as he dropped his hands to his thighs and rubbed.

"You said you think we have the wrong guy." Sam leaned back and folded his arms across his chest.

"Yeah."

"Why?"

Charlie pushed her hair back. She looked up at him with all her questions plastered on her face.

"Not sure yet, but something feels off."

His cropped hair did nothing to hide that furrowed brow.

"Okay, let's talk it through." Sam finally took a sip. "The victim was killed by a single shot to the head from close proximity. No signs of restraint suggests that he knew his killer. The method of disposal was consistent with that of the Petrović family in New York."

Charlie tilted her head in a half nod. "Not completely, but we'll get back to that."

"Dominic Ilić worked for Nicholas Mirković, associate of the Petrovićs, who also hired Andrija Durić and recently brought over Vincent Petrović; both of whom were seen with the victim the night he was murdered."

Charlie sat uncomfortably still.

"We have a witness statement that places Andy and Vince together twice that day. At the first, they were heard describing the very crime that later took place, and the second time at the dump site, forty feet below the actual crime scene."

Sam paused his recap and waited for some acknowledgement from Charlie. "Yes," she sighed.

"So, what's on your mind?"

"His feet."

Sam sputtered into his drink.

"Don't they bother you?"

"I didn't think you were squeamish."

"That's not what I meant." Charlie set her mug down a little too hard. Sam watched her silently collect herself. "It's a minor deviation, I'll give you that. But here it is significant. Why change the MO?"

Sam rubbed his chin. "We know that Vince was aware of the process back home, but we don't know that he ever did it there. This could be his variation of the technique."

"Or someone who heard the story from him."

Charlie rested her arms on the table. "I can't shake it. Yes, we have Vince but where is Andy? I find it hard to believe that Vince could mastermind anything."

Sam raised his eyebrows in agreement. Charlie continued.

"Why would Vince, immediately upon landing, not only plan on murdering one of Nick's guys, but also basically announce it, loudly in public, to Andy who had no reason to follow him. Then they get into a brawl — again publicly — with the victim that same day. And to top it off, they are seen at the scene. It's all so careless. And don't get me started on this witness."

Sam's brows snapped together, eliciting an eyebrow raise from her.

"You don't find it suspicious that this kid just so happened to find the body on the very day he'd heard them talk about it. Chicago may be small, but it's not that small." She picked at the sugar packets angrily. She couldn't get a text back, but this kid could run into the same mobsters twice in a day.

"We looked into him. Liam Broci is in no way associated with the Serbian mob, or any mob for that matter."

"You don't find that odd?" Sam tilted his head. "This kid has practically nothing. No family to speak of, no job, no money, hardly any friends," she laughed sarcastically. "Only connection in his life is this girl, who conveniently was with him at the most opportune time."

"He's got no record. He hasn't even got a speeding ticket to his name."

"He hasn't got anything," she mumbled into her drink. Charlie inhaled loudly. She couldn't find the right words to express her distrust of the kid. Most cases were straightforward. There were rarely any outliers. The pieces may be rough around the edges but they fit. But he bothered her. He was just too convenient. Charlie hung her head. Perhaps she was looking a gift horse in the mouth.

"Charlotte," Sam's tone lowered. Charlie's eyes shot up to meet his. "We have a member of a notorious crime syndicate behind bars who could lead us to get a few more on conspiracy charges. I like where your head is at, but if we pursue your line of enquiry we could lose that."

Gentle as he was, she heard his message loud and clear. Sam straightened in his seat.

"Have you had a chance to see the city?"

"Not this time," she schooled her features. "But I came here on a family vacation when I was fifteen."

"Lot more you can do now without parental supervision." He winked.

Charlie let out a shallow laugh.

Reaching the office, Charlie thanked Sam for the coffee.

"Any time," he breathed, guiding her into the building by the small of her back. She had every intention to let it go. Just one more hit of curiosity and she'd drop the matter forever. Charlie signed Liam's laptop out of evidence for one last look at his life. Sam was right, he didn't appear to have any ties to the crime family. He didn't appear to have much going on at all. He was just a kid. Liam was like sparkling water. To someone thirsty for answers, he looked like a treat but the reality left her unquenched. She chased his video with a replay of Shorty's interview. The third person in Liam's account of the store was a surly kid that went by Shorty. Officially he was a bike messenger; his deliveries were anything but. It didn't take much to loosen his lips.

"Didn't know they were going to kill Dom. Thought he was full of shit. Making himself look like a boss. Then I heard about it. Didn't make sense. Yeah, Dom was a dick - always trying to get a buck - but that was a bit much. You see what they did to his feet? That was fucked up!"

Charlie was certain that Vince should be kept away from society, but she wasn't sure if he belonged behind bars.

In her motel, Charlie was swarmed with emotion replaying the day. She quieted her thoughts climbing under those sketchy sheets. It felt good to be part of the team. She took comfort in being in on the plan. If only she could swallow that niggling feeling.

The morning did not bring a surge in confidence, but Charlie was determined not to make waves. She fixed a demure expression on her face and went about her day, determined to be content with what they had. Rosalia nearly threw a wrench in her plan.

"You were right." Her chipper voice on the phone irked Charlie.

"Don't say that."

"Don't know how you saw it, but you were right about the feet. Unlike the previous cases, there was no sign of healing and the tools differed."

"The tools?"

"The healing tells us the torture was done over time. Burns lay upon other burns." There was a lovely misplaced lilt in her voice Charlie hadn't noticed before. "I can't be sure what they used, but probably some form of pipe. This one, like I said, is explosive. Likely done by a blowtorch."

Charlie furiously tapped her pen against the table, earning the ire of those surrounding her. She should say something. They should take another look. Her brain scrambled to formulate a plan of attack. Looking around, Charlie saw Sam walk back into the bullpen. He motioned her over; her resolve weakened with every step. There was a firm finality to their handshakes. The powers that be were convinced they would secure a conviction against Vince for this. There was insufficient evidence to tie him to the New York cases. Essentially, there was no reason to stick around. Charlie took a good look at their faces. She had a feeling she'd be seeing them again.

TIP #9

REIN IN YOUR EGO

You may feel like it's you versus the world. Let it be a consolation, the world probably hasn't even noticed you.

CHAPTER 19

T
hey were fucking. James was sure of it. He suspected as much when they first arrived, but seeing them at the cafe sealed it. They were on the clock and taking the time to have a little date. Either that or they were discussing the case in private. James grimaced. He didn't know which annoyed him more.

They both thought they were so smart. Flying halfway across the country to take over such an easy case. *Waste of time and money,* James thought. His whole body was tighter than a new jar of peanut butter, which Sam could probably open on the first try. He probably didn't even have to look down at it, he'd just manage with barely a flick of the wrist. He was just there to show them all up with that cute little assistant of his.

A scowl was deeply ingrained into the contours of his face by the time he reached his desk. There were no notifications on his cell. None of his texts got replies. None of his calls got answered. James bypassed worry straight to furious. Where the hell was Andy? What was the point of him being an informant if he wasn't sharing his information?

They had returned. They weren't even hiding it. Sam and Charlie had been joined at the hip since they arrived. James wondered how literally. He kept his eyes on the skittish blonde. She looked like she was up to something. He glared at his colleagues for loudly shuffling about, he couldn't make out the nature of her phone call. Reading her lips was out of the question, as big as they were, since she faced away from him when she answered the phone. Why was she so mistrustful? She sauntered off, but returned before James could make up a reason to follow her. She checked out the male witness'

102

laptop. James scoffed. I.T. already combed through it. What was she looking for? They really were determined to waste everybody's time.

The dawn brought him a surge of confidence. Plastering on a happy face, James was determined to offer his help wherever he could. He'd suck it up to learn what they knew. Fate intervened and he saw fit to send them home early. Sam explained there were insufficient ties to the cases in New York. James happily nodded along. Really was such a waste of time. A gentle woodsy smell alerted him that Charlotte was nearby. She stood stoically on the outskirts of the assembled group. He quirked a brow in her direction. She must have felt his stare as she turned to face him.

"It was a pleasure to have you here," he sneered.

She smiled dismissively.

"What time is your flight?"

"We leave in an hour," she replied curtly.

James grinned. "I could check that laptop back into evidence for you."

Her hooded eyes narrowed at his offer.

"That's kind of you, thank you." Sam accepted on her behalf. James hadn't noticed he was paying attention. Shouldn't be a surprise, given the nature of their relationship. Sam clapped him on the back and walked off. James smirked down at Charlotte as she was led away. He'd have more time to find what she missed.

TIP #10

THERE IS NO SHAME IN STARTING OVER

Grab a pair of floaties and get back in the pool.

CHAPTER 20

I t was for the best that Liam and Stef hadn't made plans for Thanksgiving that year. They probably would have argued about where to go and what to bring. He would have tried to convince her not to go and she would have gotten upset. Stef hated calling in last minute cancellations with bad excuses. They had a good reason this year, but he was happy they didn't have to make that call. What would they even have said? *"Hey, thanks again for the invite. Sorry this is so last minute but we can't make it for dinner. Why? Because the FBI is moving us to an undisclosed location. Why? Because we make bad choices."*

"Wait here. Someone will be in shortly to explain the training and process from here on out. Can we get you anything in the meantime?"

"Tea, please." Liam asked for both of them, keeping one arm around Stef who remained stone faced.

Stef and Liam were shivering inside a nondescript building waiting to be told how badly they screwed up. Stef rubbed her arms to keep warm. Someone arrived moments later with two cups of tea. Liam thanked him and handed one over to Stef, who was barely acknowledging him. Once left alone, he spoke in hushed tones.

"I know you're still mad, but think of it this way: you never would have killed yourself."

"So you killed me instead?" She gave him a lop-sided grin.

"Shouldn't be a surprise, everyone thought we'd go out together."

"Not sure that's how they meant."

"Nope, definitely a murder-suicide pact."

Their laughter was interrupted by an agent who took them through their current predicament.

They spent a little more than a week in the facility awaiting their new lives. Their babysitter pointed out how incredibly quickly their process was moving. Even if that were true, Liam thought it was a terrible inconsiderate thing to say to people trapped in a box. The pair had no involvement in their placement and weren't kept abreast of the goings on around them. They were aware of the presence of other people, but socializing among guests was strictly prohibited. Liam had few objections as he suspected the majority were of the criminal variety. As they weren't directly involved in any criminal activity, they got fast-tracked. Early on Thanksgiving morning, the couple were pushed into a gray Camry and driven away from their old life.

Liam drifted in and out of sleep on the least fun road trip ever. Once in the car, Stef perked up.

"Is there any chance we're relocating to Nashville? I've alway wanted to go."

"No."

Marshall Aquilino was a serious man. From what Liam could see, he was as close to two dimensional as physically possible. Liam wanted to believe that was just how he acted on the job, but he blended right into the driver's seat.

"Can we at least drive through?" Stef asked hopefully.

"We're heading west."

"You say that like it's obvious."

"The sun is going to set directly in front of us."

"Okay, boy scout. It's not setting right now so we just have to take your word for it." She pouted sinking deeper in the backseat. "So far witness protection sucks."

Aquilino shook his head in contempt. Liam looked back, amused, as Stef glared daggers into the back of the Marshall's head. She met Liam's gaze and softened.

"Please change the station."

Liam obliged, ignoring the look Aquilino sent his way. He rolled his eyes at the whitening knuckles gripping the steering wheel. Tuning out the faint sounds of the car, Liam watched the landscape roll by. Hills blanketed in snow stood against a cloudy backdrop. Liam wondered if there would be snow at their destination. He tried to glance back at Stef in the mirror, but couldn't see her. Content that the Marshall was largely ignoring them, Liam turned to see Stef stretched out as best he could in the backseat. The gentle rise of her chest suggested she fell asleep. She opened her eyes and smiled. Snow be damned.

CHAPTER 21

Getting blue-balled by the Almighty is on a whole other level. Andy shifted in his seat. There was a small window to find the asshole that stole his life before he disappeared forever and Andy had no leads. To say that dampened his spirits was an understatement. The engaging beat, innuendo-laced lyrics, and lace-covered tits weren't enough to pull Andy out of his funk.

His phone lit up with another text notification. Andy ditched his main phone when he skipped town, but kept the burner phone he used to contact Mischa. He opened the message. Once again she pleaded for him to come in, going as far as to suggest admitting to their affair. He rolled his eyes and threw the phone back into his pocket. He couldn't go back. They'd kill him. Andy had to find who saw him. He could have sworn there was no one around at the time.

The woman on stage gyrated her hips in time with the last few bars of the song. He hadn't even noticed when this one came out. He'd been missing a lot lately; he chastised himself by downing another shot. Andy couldn't afford to get careless. Stepping out into the cold air, Andy watched his breath for a moment. It had been a few weeks since he met with James. If he left it any longer it would look more suspicious. He rubbed the back of his neck and walked off.

Andy didn't need to make himself look distraught this time. The lack of sleep and anger ate away at him. It was a risk to be back in the city, even in the suburban fringes. Andy kept his head down to stop himself from constantly looking back. Nick surely had people looking for him. He pressed himself into the alcove in the entryway and waited for James to buzz him in. They didn't exchange greetings when James opened the door.

"Got some leftover Chinese. You can help yourself."

Things couldn't be worse. He was being fed scraps and made to sleep on a couch. Andy didn't think he'd ever lived rough, not even after his mother kicked him out as a kid. James had the good sense not to press the issue. He didn't bother with small talk. After pointing out the location of the dishes and sheets, he went to turn in for the night.

"We'll head out early in the morning."

Andy made a non-committal gesture as he forked some gummy beef and undercooked broccoli into his mouth. Ever the civilized house guest, Andy cleaned up after himself. Not ready to coax comfort out of James' couch, he wandered the tiny space, careful not to make any giveaway sounds of snooping.

The house was tidy. Barely lived in, Andy imagined. He didn't expect to find anything of interest. James was not a particularly interesting person. His job, however, was. Pausing outside of James' room, Andy waited for any signs of life. When he was certain James had fallen asleep, Andy went straight for his satchel. It didn't contain much, just his wallet, tablet, and a laptop. Andy looked back to the table he'd sat at in confusion. Thereon, lay another laptop. Andy looked back down at the one in his hand and opened it. It was unlocked. He sat back and clicked on the folder of photographs. There were few pictures. Mostly of groups. One woman appeared frequently. Andy licked his lips and opened a picture of the same woman on the beach. Her head was thrown back in a laugh. One hand pushed back her wet curls, exposing her ample breast, tastefully contained in a black bikini top. This wasn't James' laptop. James didn't have a girlfriend. Definitely not one that pretty.

CHAPTER 22

Liam had just started getting feeling back in his legs after an eternity in the car and a ferry over choppy gray waters, but taking the stairs to his new apartment on the fourth floor made him feel them a little too much for his liking. Their early morning arrival on an island resting just off the coast of the Pacific Northwest was unmemorable. Empty streets and closed offices greeted them. The properties surrounding the squat red brick building they were marched into were in need of repainting.

Once inside the apartment, Liam crashed onto the nearest soft surface while Stef stretched out on the floor below him. Aquilino paid them no mind and launched into a lecture on security protocols. He spoke in clipped sentences, not realizing he lacked an attentive audience. Stef rifled through the bags on the floor. Liam heard the rustling of paper but didn't look over. He stared blankly at the popcorn ceiling.

"Got that," Aquilino snapped.

"Yup," Liam mumbled. "Check in, blend in, and don't tell anyone we're hiding from the mob."

In his periphery, Liam watched Aquilino pinch the bridge of his nose. The Marshall reached for his bag. His eyes widened when he found it empty then quickly narrowed upon seeing Stef flip through the folder he wanted. Quickly, he snatched it out of her hands, unbothered by her indignant gasp. Liam placed a comforting hand on her shoulder and shot Aquilino a dirty look.

"This folder contains all of your new paperwork. You've got IDs, social security cards, qualifications: everything you need to build a new life."

"Any chance there is a new credit score that goes with all that?"

Liam yelped when Stef pinched his ankle.

"It's all new," was Aquilino's reply.

A quizzical expression crossed Stef's face. "What if we're applying for jobs and they ask for a reference?"

The Marshall tapped the manilla folder. "All the contact information is in here. We have a department that covers that."

Content that he passed along all the necessary information, Aquilino left them alone. From his seat, Liam surveyed their barely furnished apartment. Stef pushed herself onto the faded green couch beside Liam, tucking a foot beneath her.

"So…food?"

Liam groaned and leaned across, draping himself over Stef's lap. The faint lines she traced on his back sent him off into a peaceful slumber.

CHAPTER 23

S tef spent the first week of her new life indoors. Liam took to exploring the island. Every day, he'd tempt her towards the door, and every day she'd wave him off through a sea of paperwork. Carefully, she combed through their new identities and all the expected documentation that came with it. She analyzed the safest ways to pay their bills, balancing minimal digital trails with the least amount of social interaction. In the evenings, when Liam returned, she'd quiz him on the details of their cover stories, which he'd respond dutifully to between describing the layout of the small town.

"There's this little restaurant near the pier. It's kind of hidden away in the basement and only seats like five tables, but it's got massive windows so it looks like you're on the water. I'd like to take you there."

Stef visibly tensed. Liam reached for her hand. He felt her relax beneath his palm. His eyes followed hers out the window where drops slowly trickled down the glass pane. The festive decorations across the street lit up, brightening the dull street.

"We probably have some time before we have to rejoin the real world."

The corners of her mouth lifted at his words.

"And," Liam continued, "we are supposed to be on our honeymoon right now."

"What did you have in mind?"

He pumped his eyebrows suggestively. The snort that escaped among her giggles made Liam join in the laughter.

"I'm just saying we should act as newlyweds."

Stef tucked her hair behind her ear, angling herself closer to Liam.

"I know what you mean," she said breathily. Loosening her hand from his, she traced the bumps that lifted along his forearm. "I have an idea."

Liam's lips parted but he stayed quiet. He turned his palm upward to stroke the underside of her arm.

"We should redecorate."

Stef wore a naughty grin. Her hand kept its place on him. The air thickened, leaving no room for laughter. Liam suppressed a smile and shook his head.

"Let's save that for later," his voice dropped.

"Got another idea?"

Liam leaned in. "Let me take you to dinner."

She nodded with a closed mouth smile that pushed out her dimples. His hand slid up to grab hers.

"We should look the part," he said rubbing his thumb over her knuckles. "I should probably get you a ring, huh?"

Stef wrinkled her nose. "I guess."

"You seem hesitant."

"I don't think rings are very 'us'. Well, at least it's not very 'me'. I've lost almost every piece of jewelry I've ever owned."

"So what's more 'us'? Branding?"

"Kind of," she replied with a tilt of the head. "How do you feel about matching tattoos?"

"Interesting." His head mirrored hers. "Any thoughts on what to get?"

"Some variation of the infinity symbol?"

"I appreciate the sentiment, but I can't risk losing my bad bitch status." Stef swatted his shoulder playfully. "How about flowers?"

"That's pretty matrimonial. What are your favorites?"

Tapping her bottom lip, she answered, "I like long stemmed flowers; like tulips or orchids. How about you?"

"I don't know," he shrugged. "I remember my mom used to love daffodils."

Stef bit her lip mid grin and grabbed her phone.

"How appropriate! More than one daffodil is meant to signify a happy partnership."

Liam slid off of his chair onto the floor, stooping in front of her on a bended knee. Taking her hands back into his, Liam smiled widely.

"What are you doing Saturday?"

CHAPTER 24

T ap. Tap. Tap tap tap tap. Tap.

Liam clenched his fist to stop his assault on the table. He walked over to the window, holding his hands behind his back, then turned around, sideswiping the coffee table. Pacing was no better. Unceremoniously, he plopped onto the couch, then quickly straightened his spine. Liam smoothed his pants legs, jumping to his feet to avoid wrangling his outfit any further. There would be no chapel, no witnesses, no rice. There might be rice if he ordered the risotto later, but if all went well, it wouldn't get thrown. It was just another day he would spend with Stef. Liam smiled to himself knowing it wasn't. That day would be different. The first of their new life together. He wanted to make it memorable. Liam pulled his phone out of his pocket. Leaning against the arm rest, he scrolled in search of a particular playlist he had made a while back. His face pulled downward. He hadn't thought to download it before and now couldn't access it without logging into his account. Liam tapped in his information and downloaded them onto his phone. Hearing steps approaching, he tucked the phone back and looked up to find Stef standing shyly in the corridor. Liam's eyes glazed over her outfit. The flared sleeves of her dress swayed beside her as she stepped forward; sounds of the chunky heel of the matching white boots were muffled by the carpet. With her hair straightened, Stef would look at home in the pages of a magazine from the seventies. Liam took his time admiring her getup.

"You like?"

He nodded. "I can't remember the last time I saw you with your hair like that."

Stef tugged on her loose locks. "Thought it would be nice to do something different."

"You look hot," he said, wetting his lips. "Not that I don't like your hair curly. You always look beautiful." He sputtered. "You look like a Bond girl like this."

Stef lowered into a half curtsey. "You look good too. You actually cut your hair."

Liam ran a hand through it laughing. "Yeah, I got it cut earlier. You like?"

Stef reached out, following the path his fingers took a moment before. "I do."

Pushing himself off the couch, Liam stood, face slightly above Stef.

"Are you flirting with me?" Her tone was playful. Looking up through her lashes, her eyes shone with hope. Liam only nodded.

"It took getting married for you to start?"

"It's socially acceptable now," he said, raising her hand to his lips. Her giggle reverberated in his chest.

Hours later, matching plastic bandages adorned their adjacent wrists. Their coats hung loosely off their shoulders as they watched the sunset from the pier. Any residual warmth from the day faded when the pink sky darkened. Liam and Stef took refuge from the biting chill in a nearby hotel. Sound of merriment pointed the way to the bar. Attendees of the party ran in the ballroom trickled into the bar, keeping the newlyweds in a steady stream of congratulatory drinks.

"What brings such a young couple out here?" A visiting pair asked them, signaling the bartender for another round.

"Property value," Liam joked.

With a quick toast, the tourists excused themselves. Alone again, Liam and Stef ventured out to the veranda. Music from the party spilled into the night. Liam wrapped his non-bandaged arm around her waist and pulled Stef in. They stood there, softly swaying like the waves below, enveloped in each other.

TIP #11

BREW YOURSELF A BIG CUP OF HONESTY

Before you assume that you're on the same page, make sure you're reading the same book.

CHAPTER 25

Stephanie.

The glaring typo stared at her mockingly. Ph. Gone was Stef. She was Stephanie now. Yoga pants were traded for slacks. No more mats on the floor, Stephanie sat in ergonomic chairs in the corners of conference rooms.

Settling in took longer than she expected. In her isolation period, Stef had sorted through the mundane aspects of life. She set a budget, squirreling away an emergency fund, made their house a little homier with extra locks and bolts, and memorized their neighbors' schedules to avoid awkward run-ins in the stairwells. She had run out of reasons not to surrender to her new reality especially when Liam rushed in with an excited flush to tell her about his new job as a junior report at the local paper. Stef's eyes bugged out of her head. She muttered to herself incoherently. It was all she could do to keep from screaming. But Stephanie didn't raise her voice. Stef might have yelled about his reckless behaviors and risking exposure so soon after settling. Stephanie, however, poured a large glass of wine and turned to chop vegetables. Liam approached cautiously, eyeing the large knife in her hands, to show her the limited readership as the paper only reached the island and three towns on the mainland. She ceased the grumbling and went easier on the drink. One heavy sigh and a couple of phone calls later, Stef got a job as a paralegal.

On her first day, a lanky man led Stef through the office, speaking like his life depended on it. His mouth moved the way a hummingbird flaps its wings. All his words blended into an imperceptible hum. Stef nodded occasionally, encouraging him to continue. Somewhere in the midst of it all was his name. Seeing as he didn't really know hers, and never would, she didn't feel too bad about missing it. Stef mentally kicked herself. At some point she promised to start to care. Just not yet. Soon after, she fell into a routine. From the moment she woke until she showered, she could be Stef. She was careful not to speak much in this short while, filling the time with stretches and meal prep.

Sitting in a staff meeting, going over the past year's budget, Stef once again mentally excused herself from the conversation. Having been there for less than three months, she wasn't contractually required to care. Shifting in her seat, Stef kept her eyes firmly on the notepad in front of her. She wasn't looking to share her pain with the others. Every so often, she'd move the pen around mindfully as if to keep herself physically in the room. Not that she could forget where she was in that chair. Stef fidgeted in her seat, searching for some level of comfort. She worried her ass might have gotten too big. Stef shook her head to erase the thought.

"You disagree?"

Someone on her left nudged her lightly. Stef turned her head to find the table looking her way.

"Sorry, what?" It must have looked like she opposed the last statement. She might have, but couldn't be sure since she hadn't heard it. Stef squinted her eyes a little. "No, sorry," she pushed her voice out of her nose. "I've got a terrible urge to sneeze."

Sympathetic nods were directed at her before the chattering continued. Someone passed a tissue across the table. Stef smiled in response. She brought it to her face, gently rubbing her nose before discarding the gum that rolled around her mouth for too long. She washed out the stale mint taste with a large sip of water.

Life got so choreographed. The same songs played on the radio. They rotated through the same recipes. Though they broke the touch barrier, frequently and repeatedly, Stef felt them skirting around each other. As long as Liam was happy, she would be accommodating. That was her plan. Liam seems to come into his own in this new life. Between the paper and his new

119

friends, Liam was flourishing. Stef tried to be rational, but there was no negotiating with the green eyed monster. Liam was better adjusted. Certain truths were hard to swallow, so she kept them out of her mouth. In a new city, with a new name and financial security, Stef felt exactly the same. It was looking more like she was her problem. As she readied for another day, entered the spare room for her stretching session. She set the mat in the corner and reached toward the ceiling. A creak stopped her movements. The mirrored closet door slowly swung open blocking her way. She kicked the door closed with her heel as she pushed a box into place to keep it shut. Stef moved back to the mat, pointedly avoiding her reflection.

CHAPTER 26

Liam considered taking up jogging. Four blocks later, he came to terms with the fact that a new identity did not come with lung or leg transplants. He returned for a half-assed attempt at a run to find Stef still doing yoga. He stopped at her doorway and watched her salute the sun. She looked more like her normal self like that. They were well into the summer, yet Liam found Stef frightfully cool. She didn't fight him on the little things. She wasn't quick with a quip. In fact, she stopped providing them altogether.

Breakfast was a rushed affair. Liam sat at the table with a half-eaten bowl of cereal. By the time Stef emerged from the shower, he was draining the last of the leftover milk. He pushed the box towards her. Shaking her head, she reached past him for a banana.

"Gonna be late."

She gave him a chaste peck. Her lips were warm like the embers left after a fire. Liam chased her mouth to deepen the kiss. She pulled away. When she left, he set about clearing the table. Putting away the cereal, Liam stared at the empty vase on the table. Stef usually kept fresh flowers there. He couldn't remember the last time it had been filled.

At the office, Liam had a whole day of nothing to look forward to. After drumming on his desk, rolling down the length of the aisle and swiveling in his chair, he'd checked off his to-do list for the morning. The rest of the team was off on a retreat, leaving Liam to man the phones. He didn't mind, having volunteered to stay, but he certainly wasn't happy either. For the first time in three days, his phone lit up. He didn't give it a chance to ring before it was at his ear.

"Busy day?" Chris' voice came out of the receiver laced with mirth. Liam sat back, swiveling once again.

"I mostly write obituaries, asking for a busy day seems pretty fucked up."

"Then you can get away for a bit."

Without hesitation, Liam grabbed his things, excusing himself to the empty desks around him. He headed up the street in the direction of the hotel restaurant.

Liam, unimpressed with her newfound Stepford attitude, found all manner of reasons to stay out of the house. At their makeshift reception, Liam struck up a friendship with Chris Sutherland, one half of the couple that joined them in celebration. Originally, from the area, Chris grew up to be a real estate developer with a penchant for sailing everywhere. He popped by occasionally to visit his aging mother between overseeing his projects along the western coast.

"So," Chris asked, setting his empty glass down. "How are you finding life out here?"

Liam swirled the remaining foam around the cup. "It's okay."

"Is that what you're striving for?" Chris leaned forward into a sun beam that illuminated his peppered hair. Liam tugged at his collar, envious of the forgotten buttons on Chris' shirt and sleeves.

"I honestly don't know anymore." Liam sighed. "I don't know if I'm cut out for journalism. Which puts me back at square one."

Two small cups of espresso were dropped off at their table.

"Why do you think that?" Chris didn't wait for the liquid to cool before taking a deep sip, halving the contents of his cup.

"I tried this before and I mostly sat around doing nothing. Then life got in the way before I could do anything about it. Now I sit around doing nothing, but I'm not that bothered to do anything about it. I'm not that curious, not like Stef. She knows everything."

Chris smiled knowingly. "How long have you two been together?"

"Oh, well," Liam harshly swallowed the bitter drink, feeling too ashamed to reach for the sugar. "It's hard to say. I mean we're married." He clumsily showed Chris his ring. They started wearing them a few weeks into Stef's new job. She had been asked out only twice, but it was enough to ruffle his feathers. In spite of her reassurance, Liam brought her to a jeweler and even got himself a matching one.

Chris laughed. "Word of advice: women remember anniversaries." He signaled for the bill. "But I had an ulterior motive for lunch today."

Liam tensed. He angled his legs away from the table, ready to run if the situation called for it.

"I've been reading some of your work. You paint a pretty picture with not much to go on. You're wasted there. I'd like to offer you a job."

Liam rested his elbows on the table, sliding his legs back underneath.

"My mom is getting on in her years and she's finding it hard to remember things." His voice broke. Liam nodded sympathetically. "I want you to put together her memoirs. I've got records, journals, and newspaper clippings about her life and time in the theater. I want you to piece them together. Make her something to help." Liam looked away from his misty eyes. "Besides," he continued clearing his throat, "if it goes well, you could ghostwrite my adventures. I was quite the sailor back in the day."

Over dinner, both Liam and Stef stayed safely in the shallow waters of small talk. He tapped maniacally on his thigh which didn't escape Stef.

"What's with you?"

"I was offered a job," Liam tried to keep an even tone. He recounted his conversation with Chris, including his offer to take them out over the long weekend.

"A rich old dude is inviting you onto his boat? Didn't they ever teach you about stranger danger, or is it only girls that are taught to be super paranoid?"

Liam scoffed. "You couldn't be more wrong."

"How so?"

"First off, it's a yacht, not a boat."

"Well," she rolled her eyes. "That changes things. No one has ever been violently murdered on a yacht before."

Stef sighed loudly. "Liam, have you thought about what will happen when we have to go back?"

He furrowed his brow. "What do you mean?"

"All of this," she motioned around them. "It's temporary. They're expecting you to go back and testify."

Liam didn't know how to respond. Her statement dragged him out like an undertow. He sat there gaping at her. Tired of waiting for a reply, Stef rolled her eyes again and brushed past him. They prepared for bed in silence. Liam furiously brushed his teeth. He kept trying to meet her eyes in the mirror. Stef kept her head down, setting her thick hair in braids. They climbed into bed without a word, the tension stitched into the sheets.

The quiet was deafening. It has been building for a while, but it had never been so palpable. Liam waited for her breathing to even out.

"I can't sleep." For a moment, he thought he imagined her voice. Liam turned his head only to be met with a blank expression. He threw their covers off which landed softly in the dark. Liam tripped over them forcing his legs into the nearest pair of pants. Stef followed suit more gracefully. Swiftly and silently, they made it out of the building in search of perspective.

A path to a hiking trail sat just outside the rear entrance. Liam meant to lead them to the cliffside, but Stef had a different plan. Not wanting to call out in the dark, Liam tried his best to stay close as she forged a path through the shrubbery. The rustling of leaves underfoot barely disguised his labored breathing as they made their way up the hill. In the clearing, they found a lighthouse. Liam perched on a rock to catch his breath while Stef tried the door.

"Stef?"

She took off around the building. He watched her peer into the windows.

"This one is open." Her whisper cut through the darkness. Liam groaned, lifting himself off his perch. Once in, Stef took off in a sprint up the stairs. Liam looked around for any sign of life. He climbed quickly, propelled by a fear of getting caught. A hefty amount of dust, kicked up by their interruption, danced in the moonlight. The place didn't get much foot traffic. Liam related his efforts until his hand brushed against a large cobweb. Shaking off any potential hitchhikers, Liam took off at double the pace.

The cool air at the top was a relief. Stef leaned precariously over the railing.

It creaked under her hands as she shifted. Liam sidled up behind her, keeping the frigid concrete tightly against his back.

"You're scowling."

His brow creased. She continued to look out at the view.

"You got eyes on the back of your head now?"

"I know you like I know the folds of my vagina." Stef turned to face him. "I don't need to see you to know something is wrong."

He stuck his tongue out at her. It dried in the arctic wind.

"But lately, I can't for the life of me figure out what you're thinking."

Liam crossed his arms.

"Could say the same thing about you."

Another gust of wind carried away her response. There were questions he wanted to ask, but he was scared of her response. He didn't know what he'd say if she turned the questions back on him. Her body shook, drawing his eyes back to her. Stef rubbed her arms, coaxing more heat out of her fleece sleeves.

"Come here." Stef stepped into Liam's outstretched arms. She tucked her head into the crook of his neck. Liam stilled his hands, pulling her a little tighter. They could talk in the morning, he decided. Over her head, Liam watched their sleepy town. Under its navy blanket, he could just about make out their red brick building. Their hideout. Their quiet corner. Their home. The windows reflected the flickering of the streetlamp below their apartment. Liam's eyes followed the light as it dawned between the windows then disappeared. He moved closer, squinting his eyes. A yellow hue filled the window then darkened again.

"Did you leave the candle on?"

Stef loosened her hold to look up at Liam.

"No," she said questioningly. She followed his gaze to their apartment. It was still. She glanced up at him but his stare did not waver. Stef looked back out. A burst of color spilled out of the top floor. A shadow moved between the windows. In his periphery, the glow of the whites of Stef's eyes let him know she saw it too.

"Any chance that's Aquilino checking up on us?" Her voice quavered.

"Doubt it."

"Should we call him?"

Liam felt Stef reach into her pocket. He tightly gripped her wrist. "I don't think so."

The shadow returned, moving slowly across the room before vanishing into the apartment. Liam didn't wait for the shadow to reemerge. He tugged Stef towards the stairs. His lungs were on fire as they took off down the cliff. He didn't care. They had to reach the docks.

TIP #12

APPROACH WITH CAUTION

Some people will tell you not to look down, to leap without looking, carpe diem...
You may notice they don't say much else. That's because they're dead.

CHAPTER 27

Framing someone for murder should have been the last straw, but Andy had always been resilient. Even he had to admit that stealing evidence from the Feds was a step too far. With the laptop, Andy had all he needed to cut ties with Chicago. Leaving James' place, Andy found a car and headed west, stopping only when both he and the car tired.

He made it to somewhere in Colorado when he decided to lie low for a bit. Andy took his time strolling through the supermarket aisles getting supplies. In all likelihood, he'd be living out of his car for the foreseeable future. He eyed the liquor but decided against it. He'd need a clear mind. Andy began to walk away when a synthetically chirpy voice got his attention. It was a tone reserved for small children and the incompetent but most certainly did not belong among those bottles.

"Did you make it to grandma's okay?" Andy scoffed, losing interest in whoever was clearly on the phone.

"Was your father driving safely? Oh, Michelle is there too?" He raised an eyebrow. "No, that's fine. Have fun and behave for grandma. I'll see you in a week."

At that, Andy turned the corner for a better look. There was only one person in that aisle, bent over looking at the selection of rosés. Her hair was piled messily on her head. A drab outfit covered her, barely disguising that shapely ass from that angle.

"Is that one any good?" Andy saw her jump, clinging tightly to the bottle she had picked out.

"I- I don't know," she stammered, smoothing her hair. "I just know it's cheap."

Andy chuckled, the woman joined in, pulling her hair down to cover her rose tinged ears. He stepped closer, trapping her body between his and the shelf.

"Try this one," he reached for a bottle just beside her. "My treat."

Her eyes widened followed by her smile.

Andy slid her the bottle after they made their respective purchases. He lingered, helping her back to her car.

"Would you like to, I don't know, share this with me later?"

Andy smirked, accepting the invitation. At least he sorted out his accommodation issue.

Dinner and drinks turned into breakfast and a free place to crash and comb through the laptop. Andy examined every folder, looking for some insight into this person. From the mountains of resumes, Andy learned his name. Broci. The half-finished cover letters told him this guy was looking for a writing job. Good chance he might still. An internet search turned up nothing but a handful of old articles but no pictures. If he wasn't so invested in killing him, Andy would have called off his search on such a boring individual. Clicking out of a window, he accidentally opened a music app. Going to close it, Andy stopped at the notification of ongoing downloads. He raised his brow at that and checked for other devices. There he was — only a couple states away.

Tempting as it was, Andy kept the laptop shut. He couldn't risk alerting this Liam asshole that he was close. He did, however, keep looking him up online. Still nothing. No news articles, no social media, nothing. It dawned on him that he might have changed his name, but Andy wasn't discouraged. He may not have a name or a picture, but he had an address. With no one else on the road, Andy smoothly backed into a spot right in front of his destination. Worn out as he was from the thirty-seven hour drive, he didn't want to let that building out of his sight. He was determined to keep his eyes on the door but a blink got out of hand.

Sun bled through his eyelids without any of the accompanying warmth. Andy awoke annoyed. He wrestled movement out of his stiff fingers. The building stood before him, an angry red in the light of day. Andy's joints groaned when he sat up. The entrance once again held his full attention until his bladder painfully called it away. Not willing to turn his back on the building, Andy had no choice but to go against it. He crossed the road quickly, the cold morning mist seeping into his bones. Assured by the lack of movement in the early hour, he relieved himself beside the dumpsters. His muscles relaxed as a loud steam smacked the wall. Sudden footsteps startled him, sending the last drops all over his hands. The warm liquid cooled instantly on his skin. Andy waited for the passerby but the steps quieted. He wiped his hands on his trousers and continued rubbing them the whole way back to the car. Back inside, a deep sigh fogged his view but he refused to turn the engine on. He reached in his bag in the backseat for another sweater which he roughly pulled on, curling into himself before looking out over the steering wheel. Sleep wasn't done with him under the extra layers. Andy fought it but a couple raps on glass told him he had lost.

"You alright in there?"

Andy blinked hard. An elderly man stood at the window.

"Yeah," he sat up. "Carpool, you know?"

The man nodded and turned away. Just past him, Andy watched people ruffle inside the door. He swore. It was brighter now and the street was more active. People swarmed in the cafe in his rearview mirror. He gave in and hurried inside. Plopping into a seat in front of the large window, Andy slid on the plastic cover. He wrapped his hands around the steaming mug and continued his watch. Grumbling, he accepted refills, turning down attempts at conversation with a blank stare. Nothing of interest passed by until the door swung open again. It was her. The woman from the pictures.

Andy debated following her. It was too risky and he needed to see his energy. He just needed to find a place to wait for her return. Andy found his way into the building across the street. It was shorter, but from the roof he could look into all of the apartments. Making his way through the halls, he stopped at a door with a large pile of mail and deliveries spilling over the welcome mat. With a cursory glance around, Andy forced the door open and made himself at home. The apartment was chaotically decorated. Every surface was covered with mismatched knickknacks. The floors had to be carefully navigated from the sculpted bobbles strewn about. He didn't bother giving any of it a proper look. Andy headed straight for the bed. He set an alarm and promptly collapsed.

The sky was darkening when he resumed his watch. He sat at the window, covered by the dusty curtains. The streetlights hadn't yet turned on when he caught sight of her. Andy raced to the roof when she disappeared into the building. Moments later, movement on the fourth floor caught his eye. He watched her mill about the place. Despite that figure, she was unremarkable. Yet he couldn't look away. Just after night fell, another figure appeared. Andy sat up, anger coursing through him. That must be him. He tried to get a better view, but they drew the blinds and he went back inside. The curtains inside the apartment hung loosely, giving him an unobstructed view of their windows. Andy cracked open a beer. Now that he knew where they were, he could take his time and plan out his next steps.

He took a seat on the sofa he had rearranged to face the window. One bottle was followed by another which preceded a few more. None of them loosened the knot between his shoulders. Andy rubbed his neck roughly, chafing the skin there. He tried to reach lower but growled in frustration, unable to get at the painful muscle. It shouldn't have been like that. He shouldn't have had to sleep in a car or hide in apartments with no heating. He should be the one in that apartment, living a new life, free from the mess he left behind in Chicago. The lights went out across the street. He should be the one preparing for a good night's rest without a worry in the world. Those thieves had taken it from him. Andy reached for another bottle. His fingers dipped into each hole of the cardboard carton and came up empty. Six bottles lay at his feet. Glass clinked against itself and he stood abruptly, knocking the bottles out of his way. In the bathroom, he splashed water on his face, wincing as the cold touched his skin. He buried his face in a mildewy towel, sneering as the smell lingered in his nostrils as he returned out front to pace the freezing room. The walls around him were cluttered with paintings and photos. He felt the size of the room shrink from the sheer amount of stuff it contained. Andy stalked back to the window. Most of the homes across the way were blacked out. Fewer people moved about below. He was a grotesque figure where he stood keeping watch until the late hour well and truly cleared the streets. Once the last headlines dimmed from view, Andy dashed to the door, determined to end his misery.

Up on the fourth floor, Andy pressed his ear to the door on the left. Satisfied with the lack of movement inside, he jimmied the door open. Andy let the door close behind him with the softest of clicks and waited. He pulled off his boots and left them at the entrance. Crossing the carpeted living room, Andy made a stop in the kitchen. The hum of the dishwasher masked the rattle of the silverware drawer as he eased it open and fumbled with its contents. He wrapped his hand around the handle of a large knife. The carpet cushioned his feet as he made his way through the corridor. He pushed the first door open, adjusting his grip on the knife. Little light bled through the blinds, but it was enough to see the covers laying off the bed and clothes littering the floor. He moved to the second room. All furniture has been pushed against a wall leaving plenty of room for exercise equipment. But no user. The door to the bathroom was ajar. He kicked it open wider, once again revealing no one. Andy angrily flicked the light switches in every room, taking less care with the noise he made. They had been there. He moved to the wide windows in the living room, certain he'd spent the day looking from the other side. There was no movement below. Andy kicked the green couch repeatedly.

God fucking dammit.

TIP #13

KEEP PERSPECTIVE

Some problems feel like the end of the world. Some actually are.

CHAPTER 28

The cold air couldn't permeate his skin. Anger bubbled too hot underneath. The weather had yet to improve and James' mood followed suit. The intruders had long gone, his caseload had moved on, but Andy had disappeared on him. Again. After shielding him from a murder charge, opening his home to him, and even feeding him his leftovers, this was the thanks he got. Ditched and robbed. It just proved no one could be trusted anymore. Andy left James holding the empty bag. He had probably pawned it on his way out of town. James didn't have the time to track it down. He waited with bated breath for someone to notice. With the case building against Vince, the prosecution, preparing for his arraignment, anticipated the next steps and took custody of all relevant evidence. The remainder, including the witness' property, was sent off to storage without further incident. James breathed a heavy sigh of relief. He bought himself some time to remedy the laptop-sized gap.

Caffeine was forfeit. James no longer needed it to stay alert. The last few months had been a tortuous exercise in staying alert. He kept his ears open for any suggestion of suspicion. James had yet to find a replacement for the laptop. He wondered if it was even worth it. Its absence hadn't been noted, and drawing attention to it at this stage was probably counter-intuitive. But he could not get the damned thing out of his head. He was risking a reputation as an office gossip the way he snuck up on all small gatherings. His name wasn't used more than usual in a worrying fashion. There was a rise in references to 'the nosy bastard' and 'creep' but he could live with those. He just wanted them to have the decency to suspect him to his face.

James sat in the parking lot waiting for the other cars to leave before slamming on the gas. He extended the ride home checking every car in the rearview mirror. Content he wasn't being followed, James pulled his car into a spot below his window.

In the shadows of the lamplights, James walked hurriedly, propelled by a full bladder. Bursting as he was to get through the door, he could not make it in. Either a new neighbor or unwanted guest blocked his way to the keypad. James bounced in place as the poor sucker buzzed to no answer. Obnoxiously clearing his throat got drowned out by the buzzer.

"Do you mind," James asked briskly. The man didn't move.

"Hey," James clapped the man on the shoulder. "Buddy." He looked over his shoulder; his hood hid most of his face. James didn't manage to get another word out before large arms wrapped around him from behind. He tried to break free, but darkness followed a sharp pinch on his neck.

Slumped forward where he sat, James felt heavy. An ache ran down his neck. He could ease it if only his head didn't weigh a ton. Making use of his arms only revealed he was bound to a chair. The fog lifted just enough to make him aware of sounds, but it all sounded like he was underwater. Among the muffled noises, James could make out voices. He kept his head down, taking in as much of his surroundings from the limited perspective as he could.

A pair of solid black boots passed in front of him and out of view. A gravelly voice came from somewhere behind. The boots returned and stopped at his feet; its laces caught underneath the heel. James winced, closing his eyes tightly, when grabbed by the hair. A fist threw his head back. Heat radiated from where he was struck. Through the ringing, the voices sounded closer. In the midst of the insults, they yelled indiscernible questions. James could only answer in pained groans. A blow to the stomach suggested their dissatisfaction with his reply. James gasped to catch his breath. The boots stomped off. In his ear, the course voice spoke.

"Where is he?"

"Who?" James managed through a clenched jaw. A warm drop trickled down his cheek. He couldn't be sure whether it was sweat or blood.

"Andy, you dumb fuck." A finger jabbed him in the ribs.

James shook his head, trying to straighten up. "I don't know," he spat. His nose cracked under the man's fist. His eyes watered violently, joining the other liquids on his face. There was no reprieve as a flurry of punches aimed at his head, chest, and abdominals followed quickly. The nausea worsened. Jame could no longer make out their words over the roar of blood in his ears. The assault came to a sudden stop. They walked off, leaving James whimpering in his seat. The painful throbbing lulled into unconsciousness.

Drifting in and out, James caught the odd phrase. From the little he captured, he got the gist of the story. There wasn't much to go on, but "Andy run if," "Vince couldn't wipe," and "find him" wasn't too hard to put together, even in his state. James heard them approach. He refused to lift his head. A steady stream of air was interrupted by a series of clicks. An orange flame cut through all other noise. Realization had James scrambling to wrap his feet around the legs of the chair. He weeped openly when strong hands pulled his shoes off.

CHAPTER 29

Protected persons or not, he was going to kill them. Fury propelled Aquilino up the stairs. The idiots missed their scheduled meet up and didn't even have the courtesy to answer his calls. He desperately hoped they were just inconsiderate assholes. If they were alright, he'd kill them. If they weren't ...

He had been to their offices first. The newsroom was a dead end. No one seemed to work there. The first was no better. A man with a terrible comb-over spoke a hell of a lot, but hadn't said anything useful other than the girl stopped showing up a few days ago.

Each step across the landing was cushioned with worry. Aquilino unholstered his weapon at their door. He kicked the door in after a cursory knock. It had been locked but not bolted. He hoped that meant they were just out. He called out and got silence in reply. The apartment looked undisturbed. Plates stood drying on the dish rack. The sink was spotless. He moved inward. The bedroom was empty. Bedsheets clung tightly to the bed. His shoes sunk into the clean carpet as he went to check the closet. Clothes hung neatly. Next he tried the bathroom. If anything was out of place, Aquilino couldn't tell. The towels hung crisply on the railings. A stray droplet refused to drop from the shower-head. Something about its stillness unnerved him. He backed out and into the spare room. All items, pushed against the wall, cleared a path to the closet, the door of which was slightly ajar. He tightened his grip on his gun.

Throwing open the door, he took aim inside. Empty. Aquilino exhaled deeply. Closing the door, he was faced with himself in the mirror. Over his reflection's shoulder, he locked in with a pair of blue eyes.

TIP #14

TRUST YOUR GUT

Regret, injury and ruined pants: what you can expect from ignoring your gut.

CHAPTER 30

A deep shudder shook Charlie as she stepped back into the office. Chicago welcomed her back with a chill and dread. She couldn't remember it having been this cold the last time. Making her way across the floor, Charlie blamed the air conditioning that bit at her bare ankles, turning a blind eye to the glares that followed them to the conference room. Upon the news of Horne's murder, Sam rushed them back to assist. Charlie wondered if he had even considered whether their assistance was even wanted.

She took her seat upfront beside Sam. The room filled slowly. Charlie bounced her leg, frustrated at the apparent lack of urgency. Sam rested his large hand on her knee, stopping her fidgeting. He didn't see her irritation, merely withdrawing his hand as her glare pierced the side of his face. Charlie turned back, staring blankly ahead. It was all she could do to ignore the rising heat from the eyes burning into her back.

There was no doubt his death was related to Vince. Had they not rushed the first time, Horne might still darken their doorways. Guilt marred their faces as agents filed back out into the hall, leaving the supervisors to convince the prosecutors to carry on. All of the evidence they had been so sure of now seemed too circumstantial. It all rests on the witnesses. With a huff, Charlie marched down to evidence.

Charlie paced the small room waiting for approval for her request to sign out the witnesses' possessions.

"You want the whole box?" The disinterested woman behind the computer asked to her screen.

"No, just his laptop."

Bored eyes peered over the monitor.

"Please," Charlie added.

"There's no laptop registered here."

Charlie's eyes narrowed.

"Can you find where it is?"

Without a word, the woman slowly punched in keys. Charlie crossed the shoebox of a room. She stood a hair's breadth away from the wall as clacks from the keyboard continued to fill the space. The tapping got increasingly furious. Charlie, lost in thought, enjoyed the sudden silence.

"Looks like it didn't get checked into storage with the rest of his stuff."

"Can you see who had it last?" Charlie pressed herself to the desk. The record keeper folded her arms sitting back. She looked Charlie plainly in the face, searching for something. Charlie shook her head questioningly.

"Well?"

"You did."

Sharp breaths punctuated her every step. That son of a bitch never returned the laptop for her. Her short legs burned carrying her back to the bullpen. She spotted the lead investigator rounding the corner from the restrooms. Exhaling deeply, Charlie approached, softening her features. "Greyson?"

The agent stopped in her tracks. Had she been five inches shorter, it would have been like looking in a mirror.

"Sorry to hear about Horne. Please let me know if there is anything we can do to assist your investigation."

Agent Greyson nodded. Her cold brown eyes looked past Charlie to the door. Charlie moved out of her way.

"Did you find the extra laptop at Horne's place?"

Greyson turned on her heel, tilting her head at Charlie.

"The one he checked out of evidence." She continued, noting Greyson's blank face. "It belonged to the witness in the Petrović case. I just went to get it, but looks like he hadn't brought it back in."

Greyson shook her head. Her blonde hair danced around her face.

"Didn't find anything like that."

"Huh," Charlie sighed, quaking an eyebrow. "You guys pull his phone records yet?"

The agent looked Charlie up and down. "Yeah," she said after a pause. "Just got them."

Charlie waited for her to continue. "Anything interesting?"

"Don't know." Greyson placed her hands on her hips.

"Haven't gone through them yet. I'm kind of busy."

Charlie's nostrils flared at her condescending inflection.

"Can I be of assistance," she asked sweetly.

Greyson rolled her eyes. "I guess." She pulled the door open and waited for Charlie to walk through.

Hidden away at a desk in the corner, Charlie poured over Horne's phone records. Wrinkled gum rolled around her mouth. Her tongue traced the grooves. Charlie pictured a brain as she crossed off the checked numbers. She folded the gum between her teeth to smooth it out. A rushed asterisk marked another call to an unregistered number. Misshapen points dotted the paper. Pages of messages held nothing of interest until the same unknown number kept popping up. At first glance, it was nothing more than Horne getting ghosted. Charlie was ready to dismiss it when a familiar name caught her eye. Andy. Papers rustled beneath her hands as she laid them out across the desk to highlight the dates. Everything other than those ten digits faded from view. The neon yellow consumed her; Charlie took no notice of the movement around her.

"Charlie?"

Sam peered down at her. Charlie pressed the gum between her molars and followed him into the conference room. Sam leaned against the table. He crossed his arms and kept his eyes on the floor. Charlie chose to stand by the door evening out their heights.

"Prosecution is ready to drop this." His jaw tightened. "The details are too similar to Dom's case. They don't think pushing it as a copycat will help."

'We have CCTv footage of Vince at the scene."

"Barely. Between the fake cameras installed by shops and city wide budget cuts there are a few blindspots. The alley in question falls in one. We can see Vince in the car approaching the alley, but not actually in it. All we really have are the witness statements."

"About him — "

"Jesus, Charlie! Would you let that go?" We have no reason to doubt him. I just told you he's all we got."

"I know," she said, raising her voice. Sam's eyes widened. "I was going to say that he only saw them walking out afterwards. We all assumed Vince was the triggerman because of his connection to New York. What if he wasn't?"

Sam stared at her. "You think Andy?"

"It makes more sense than Vince if you think about it. We know Dom liked to extort people. Vince hadn't been here long enough to get blackmailed, but assume Andy was. What if Andy took advantage of the fight to get Vince to come along? He could then use his MO and leave him to take the blame."

Sam ran a finger across his lips. She continued before he could speak. "Look, I also found this. Horne had semi-frequent contact with this one unregistered number that could be Andy."

Sam grabbed the papers from her hand. "You think Andy killed Horne?"

"You remember the laptop I checked out back in December?" Sam nodded. "Horne said he'd take it back for me since we had to rush to the airport." He nodded again. "Horne never checked it back in. The rest of the witness' things went into storage, but not the laptop. And they didn't find it in his apartment either."

Excitement danced in her eyes. Finally, she felt like she was catching up. Sam shot up.

"So where is the laptop?"

"Not sure," she said, shaking her head. "But I'm willing to bet that Andy has it."

Sam rushed to the door. "We need to call the Marshalls."

CHAPTER 31

Details of the Marshall assigned to the witnesses came after a few calls and shouting matches that Charlie watched through the glass doors. It hadn't been the break they hoped for, as his name came with an approximate time and cause of death.

Sam stormed past Charlie, leaving her to pry the story out of someone else. In her periphery, she watched him punch a number into a phone. Not wanting to miss any more, Charlie cautiously inched closer to where he stood bellowing into the receiver. Keeping a safe distance meant she missed the who and where of the person on the other end.

"You heard about this Aquilino murder?"

Charlie moved closer, content it wasn't a private call. There was a lack of chairs in that part of the room. Charlie had to drag a free one from two tables away. She hadn't missed much as Sam stopped barking questions down the phone. Whoever he got on the line was either incredibly detailed or the world's slowest talker. The scowl in his handsome face deepened. Charlie stopped her fidgeting and sat up straight.

"Alright, keep me posted."

Hanging up, Sam made a grotesque figure hunched over the desk.

"CCTv from a bank near the dump site caught Andy skulking around the building the Marshall was last seen entering."

Blood drained from Charlie's face. "What about the witnesses?"

"There's no trace of them. They put out an APB including their new aliases but so far nothing."

Charlie huffed. "I'll see if we can track any bank activity.

With any luck, their disappearance is unrelated."

Sam narrowed his eyes at her. Disappointment turned him into a petulant child. Charlie caught herself about to roll her eyes. She was going to need piping hot moral support. A mug sat untouched for hours, judging by the curdled residue scumming the top. She reached to take it away.

"Leave it," he growled. Shrugging in resignation, Charlie left.

INTERLUDE

You'll win some, you'll lose someone.

CHAPTER 32

In the middle of the night, dainty feet pattered on thick carpet. Darkness filled the empty hallway as she made her way through with a guiding hand on the velvety wallpaper. Mischa appreciated the dark. It hid the ugliness in her life. She moved faster; the friction reddened her fingertips. The discomfort barely registered.

Carpet gave way to cool tiles. Flicking on the lights, she didn't worry about disturbing anyone on this end of the house. Mischa threw open the fridge doors, taking stock of its contents. Her skin welcomed the cold air. She filled her arms with things to mend her broken heart. Nudging the doors closed with her hip, she caught a sharp corner and yelped. It was the first time in ages she heard her own voice.

A good little doll. That's all she was to them. It was easily done. Stay silent, stay pretty, and play stupid. Mischa didn't mind. The less they thought of her, the less time she had to spend with them. At twenty-one, she happily traded a personality for Louis Vuitton. Back then she had never heard of depreciation, but it didn't matter. She was content. Mischa had far more than she had growing up. She got farther than her father expected. Having a pretty daughter stopped being a burden when all his bills got paid. Her mother never stood up for her, but even her silent disapproval diminished with every trip to the salon. Still, they treated her the same, only tempering their criticisms when it came time to foot the bill.

Marrying Nick brought more of the same. Whether it was to open her legs or her wallet, everyone wanted something from her and they expected it with quiet obedience. And she gave it. Mischa didn't have anything of her own, so she willingly played by the rules of others to enjoy their things. It was fine. It had been until Andy came along.

He had always been around. He sat among the others, and showed her respect when Nick was around. Unlike the others, he didn't make lecherous comments as soon as her husband was out of earshot. He didn't look at her like a piece of meat. He just looked at her.

It should have been just sex. Something just for herself. There was nothing she could give him he couldn't get elsewhere, and he asked for as much. His silent attentiveness was more than she thought to ask for. Years of being ogled at and finally someone saw her. Andy brought feeling back into her number heat and, like a fool, she began to hope. Mischa dreamed of a life for them, a safe space where they could be free. She got a new lease on life only for him to be presumed dead. He was as good as if he ever showed up.

At first she tiptoed around, waiting for the other shoe to drop. If Nick had him killed, she was sure to follow. She listened intently for news when her messages bounced back. The simple fact was that he was gone. He abandoned her and everyone else soon followed. Her husband turned his attention to other women. The others gave her sour complexion a wide berth. Again, she didn't mind. Mischa had no heart left to break.

Realizing her phone would never flash his name again made her stomach fall out of her ass, leaving a bottomless pit no amount of chocolate could fill.

TIP #15

BE CONSIDERATE OF OTHERS

Regardless of your belief system, all texts condense to "don't be a dick."

CHAPTER 33

In his former life, Liam hadn't had the chance to spend much time on boats. He had the right idea then. Two days into their voyage with Chris, Liam leaned over the side of the yacht, feeling a little less like death. A warm body sidled up to him.

"So," Stef looked straight ahead at their sparkling blue surroundings. "Is witness protection all you imagined?"

Liam lifted his head enough to side-eye her before letting it roll back down. He hurt too much to bother with a sarcastic laugh.

"Well, what's next? We can't reach Aquilino. Hell, we can't even be sure we can trust him. And we definitely can't go back to Chicago." Stef angled herself to him. "Do you realize we don't even have names right now?"

"Just assume your realizations are dawning on me in real time."

Stef scoffed. "I guess we get to pick new names. That must be a record."

"Nah," Liam spit overboard, content the dry heaving ceased. "I think the guy from the Leonardo DiCaprio movie still has us beat."

"Fine, but we are in the running for the world record for fuck ups."

Liam shuffled, resting his elbows on the railing. "At least I have that to fall back on."

"Ahem," Stef cleared her throat. "We. We have that to fall back on."

Another wave of nausea hit Liam hard. "You could always go back into law," he groaned.

Stef stared at him incredulously. "I lied to the FBI and escaped from witness protection. I don't stand much of a chance in front of the character and fitness board."

"That's a thing? I thought you were all professional liars."

"Yeah, but there is still an ethics committee."

Liam pushed off the railings and grumbled the two feet to the closest deck chair. He struggled to get his bearings. Burdened by a hangover he did nothing to deserve made planning their next steps difficult and Stef was doing nothing to help. He could understand her frustration, but it's not like he could have planned for the murderous psychopath tracking them down. Gentle footsteps passed him. Liam cracked one eye open. Stef sat cross-legged across from him. Liam shoved a cushion over his face to block out the optimistically clear sky.

"Remind me again how jumping aboard a stranger's boat was a good idea."

"For the last time, it's a yacht." His annoyance was only minimally muffled by the pillow.

"Right, because the important thing is naval terminology."

Liam shot up, causing bile to rise dangerously up his throat.

"If you haven't noticed, I haven't got a plan. Getting us away from the psycho killer was kind of as far as I got. I don't know what the future holds."

"Like death at sea."

"You know what? You take over. Clearly I can't be trusted to make decisions."

"That's the first smart thing you've said in months."

Liam tightly pressed his lips together and swallowed hard.

"This isn't what I had in mind."

"What exactly were you expecting?"

"Something," he hesitated, "else. More freedom I guess."

"Freedom," she repeated mirthlessly. "We lied to the FBI to afford rent. You thought that comes with freedom?"

"It was a means to an end." He ran a hand through his hair.

"What end?" She strained her voice to keep from yelling.

"What do you want? Do you even know?"

Liam's head was exploding. "If this was such a stupid idea, why did you even come? You didn't have to go along with it!"

Stef's eyes widened and her mouth followed suit. She planted her feet on the deck, fists closed firmly at her sides.

"So I was supposed to let you get arrested for obstruction of justice? You do know lying to the feds is a crime, right?"

"So you were saving me?" His eyes narrowed.

She responded with a raised brow. Its pointed arch mocked him.

"And here I thought I was doing you the favor."

"Leaving my life and everyone I know is a favor?" Her voice climbed in disbelief.

"What life?" He couldn't swallow the poison in time. "Seriously, what did you have back in Chicago?" Liam stood in front of her listing off on his fingers. "You had no job prospects other than the gym, definitely no family and those friends," he laughed. "Do you really think they even noticed we've been gone? The only relationships you had were with me and Frankie, who you barely dated, and can't see since her fiancée hates you."

He finished spewing and looked at her with hard eyes. His chest heaved. Liam kept his head high ready for whatever she'd throw back. He wasn't ready for her silence. He really wasn't ready for her to turn away. His stomach had been emptied for a while but he felt sicker than before watching her walk away.

There was hardly a trace of her. Liam rounded corners carefully, hoping to run into her. He entered rooms sniffing for lingering remains of her perfume only to find all traces had been washed away by the sea air.

Liam dined with Chris and his wife, May, lamely excusing Stef's absence. His attempts at being social stalled with every glance he stole at the empty chair. Liam couldn't remember what they said. He couldn't remember what they ate, not that he ate much of it. The draught from the vacant seat beside him took up all of his attention.

The walk back to their room was tortuous. The water beneath him calmed, not that his feet got the hint. Liam hovered by the door, debating the merits of knocking versus just walking in. Agonizingly slowly, he turned the knob. A wave of relief washed over him upon seeing her curled form on the bed. Liam wanted nothing more than to crawl in behind her and whisper his apologies into her hair. A sob shook her unconscious body, cutting him down to size. Loam took his place on the couch, not bothering with a pillow or blanket. He stared up at the ceiling, not sure if he ever drifted off.

Here lies Liam.

Asshole.

CHAPTER 34

At some point during the night, Stef's body decided to stay curled in one position, quite early on, judging by the aches she woke with. Stef rolled over with a muted whimper only to find the other side of the bed untouched. Relief battled disappointment. She perched on the end of the bed, rolling her neck to loosen those muscles. A snore from the back of the room startled her. Liam lay prone on the sofa. She watched him, noting the lack of comforts. He was bound to wake in worse shape than her. Recalling his mood yesterday, Stef quickly grabbed a chance of clothes, not wanting to be there for a repeat.

She hated that boat. The never-ending ocean was a stifling view. There were only so many places to go when avoiding everyone on board. She had too much time to think and she didn't trust her brain anymore. Thinking hadn't helped much before.

Stef had been praised for her intellect from an early age. Perhaps she got too used to it. Maybe even thrived on it. Then the compliments stopped rolling in. Here she was, years later, with nothing to show for it. Tears prickled her eyes. Stef straightened her back and went down into the galley to drown these feelings in an obscenely large mug of tea.

Blowing on her cup, Stef nestled into a corner of the elegant sitting room. She expected little to no foot traffic, so she'd be safe from prying eyes. She got through three quarters of her cup when May flitted in. White linen casually floated around her. Flowers nearly spilled out of her arms. Stef eyed them curiously. They couldn't be fresh. Where would they be stored in the middle of the ocean? May neatly arranged them into a tall crystal vase that refracted colorfully on the table. Admiring the woman's profile, Stef envied her golden hair smoothly pinned up.

"I hope you're feeling better."

May turned to Stef, whose surprise stuck to her face. She nodded in response before hiding behind the large mug.

"Dinner was dull without you."

Stef unfolded herself and went to stand by the table.

"I'm sure it was fine."

May hummed, snipping the end of a stem.

"My husband can certainly fill the silence, but Liam didn't seem so keen to keep up. It fell to me to listen to that man." She smiled mischievously. "That's why I like having you both on board. It gives me a break from being his audience."

Stef let out a half-assed attempt at a laugh.

"Don't get me wrong," May continued. "Were he any less lively, I probably wouldn't have stuck it out this long — or married him for that matter. But you can see why I'd appreciate some company while we drift at sea for three months. Sure, he's got business down the coast all summer. A normal person might just drive or, God forbid, fly. But not Chris." She smiled conspiratorially. "You know all about it. Fellow weirdo lover." She nudged Stef playfully. A genuine smile eased on to her face.

"You don't mind?"

May shrugged into her arrangement. "It was an adjustment at first. But he is a fish. Chris couldn't grow in a glass tank. At least this way I can keep him out of trouble."

"I get that," Stef mumbled into her drink.

"He needs you." May spoke softly into the flowers.

"I don't know about that." Stef crossed her arms defeated. May laid a gentle hand over hers.

"I do." She turned back to an errant leaf. "They have trouble saying it. Sometimes you have to read between the lines."

"How do I know I'm not just filling in the blanks? I feel like I'm trying really hard to see something that's not there."

"Don't go looking for proof, darling. Love isn't a science. Learn to be satisfied with what is there."

Stef played with a loose petal until the softness rolled into pulp between her fingertips.

"It would be nice to hear it."

"Yes," May nodded, "it would."

The prospect of drowning in a hot shower was so attractive, but she'd settle for just washing away the puffy face. Stef firmly shut the door to their room behind her and reached for the hem of her shirt then reconsidered. She decided to sweat out her frustration first.

Moving into her second stretch, she felt him standing beside her. Stef kept her eyes closed and continued. He said nothing, but his labored breathing told her that he was following along. Without a word, Stef guided them through the workout. Lying flat on her back, all of her emotions bubbled to the surface, leaked out of her eyes and stained her cheeks. Warmth enveloped her hand. Liam gently dragged her thumb over her wrist. She couldn't bring herself to pull it away or turn it over.

"I'm sorry."

Stef kept her eyes closed. "Why am I here?" she whispered. Stef could feel his eyes boring into the side of her face. A short burst of air tickled her temple when he moved closer to her. "I don't get you, Liam. You said you wanted a fresh start. So why did you bring me along?"

His hand ran up her arm and encircled her waist. He held her loosely but it was enough to make her lip tremble again.

"I don't know what I'd do without you."

His lips brushed against her skin when he spoke. Stef wanted to face him, but her body would not comply.

"You weren't happy in Chicago. You seemed alright on the island, but then you started talking about leaving again. I feel like I'm just waiting for you to realize you're sick of me too."

Liam maneuvered an arm under her shoulder cradling her. "I wouldn't leave you." His voice was earnest. She could picture his hooded eyes all sincere.

"Wouldn't you?" She finally opened her eyes. Though resting on his shoulder, she looked past him to the door.

"You went to the police behind my back. What's stopping you from walking away now?"

Liam lifted her chin and nuzzled her forehead.

"I need you." He kissed her temple. "But more than that," he lowered to kiss her cheek. "I really like you."

Stef's eyes fluttered. Softly, he pressed his nose to hers. She leaned into his neck.

"Stef."

He breathed her name just over her face. Liam closed the distance between them. A quiet desperation bloomed as they deepened the kiss. Liam broke away, his eyes brimming with questions. She swallowed them, reclaiming his lips.

TIP #16

PATIENCE IS A VIRTUE

Make good use of your time while you wait.

CHAPTER 35

Andy sat eerily still except for his thumb that slid along the side of his index finger as though praying the rosary.

His eyes trailed over the photo he swiped from the apartment. That was him. The one that ruined his life. Unremarkable. A forgettable nobody unravelled his perfect plan. Never had anyone tested his patience like that insolent shit. The kid wasn't even doing it on purpose, which angered Andy all the more. The fates were helping him fuck Andy over. What had he done to earn God's favor? Andy racked his brain for what he had done to lose it.

He pressed a key, waking the computer up. Once again, he refreshed the page. Nothing. The date and location of the last login remained unchanged. The coward must have realized Andy was nearby and ran. He waited around the apartment in hopes he would return. Instead, Andy nearly came face to face with a US Marshall. Rolling his body in the shower curtains, Andy thought about how differently their relationship could have been. They might not have been friends, but they could have been civil. At the very least, Andy might not have had to kill him. But there he was, disposing of a body and taking off again. Potentially being identified was bad enough, but a dead federal agent made it too risky to stick around.

Andy watched the greying walls, all too aware of each passing day. Every minute felt an eternity in this limbo. He had no appetite, not that it mattered much since every calorie he consumed was burned away by his seething. Andy hated depending on others. Yet, there he was, entirely depending on the stupidity of this kid.

TIP #17

PLAN AHEAD

Hope for the best but prepare for the worst, especially if you have the tendency to be stupid.

CHAPTER 36

L iam's eyes travelled miles up and down Stef's legs. The book in his hands went ignored in favor of the half-dressed woman across the room. After baring their feelings, their bodies followed; Liam and Stef found little need to stay clothed except for the occasions that hunger got too demanding. On one such event, Liam accepted Chris' business proposal, which led to the couple essentially moving into the library, which was nothing more than an isolated storage room containing a labyrinth of boxes. In spite of May's protests to the location, Liam and Stef took full advantage of the privacy it afforded.

She was hard at work cataloging the contents of the boxes. Liam skimmed the elegant penmanship in the diary. His eyes easily strayed from the curves on the page to the ones on Stef. Her t-shirt barely reached the top of her thighs. Sudden movements would lift to quickly flash her barely-there underwear. She turned to find his blown-out eyes following her around the room, hypnotized by the sway of her hips. Liam raised an eyebrow hopefully, ready to abandon his efforts.

"Get back to work," she ordered cheerfully, not bothering to hide her smile. Liam saluted, picking up the journal.

When the stretches between sunset and sunrise got longer, they found themselves docking more frequently. Both Liam and Stef were grateful for the chance to replace the essentials, having left everything behind. Not wanting to raise any suspicion about their lack of belongings, Liam negotiated a cash advance for his work. If the Sutherlands had any misgivings about the pair, they kept it to themselves. The freedom to buy their way to normalcy appeased Liam only slightly. Opting to keep the honest communication going, he confided his worries to Stef about starting from zero upon returning from a shopping trip. They crashed on the couch opposite their bed, leaving everything still in the bags. She squeezed the hand he kept on her thigh.

"We won't be starting exactly from zero."

Liam ran a hand through his hair. "It's like you said, we don't even have names."

"We can sort that out when we arrive. How hard can it be to get fake IDs? High school kids do it all the time. Plus we got your advance and thirty thousand dollars to get started."

Liam's brows knitted together. Stef bit her lip sheepishly.

"I might have gotten a little paranoid when we got to the island." She sighed deeply. "So I may have stored some of that WitSec money and some of my salary onto these prepaid cards. Just in case." She slid plastic cards out of random slots of her wallet.

Liam looked at her incredulously. "I could kiss you."

"You better."

CHAPTER 37

Productivity was at an all time low. Computer screens reflected glazed eyes where people stared just a little too hard. Fingers hovered over keyboards, never quite falling into a rhythm. The pretense of being busy did not disguise that everyone was acutely aware that Vince was lumbering his way to freedom.

No amount of insistence or pleading could convince the State not to drop the case. No witnesses, no accomplice, and no motive left them with an abundance of reasonable doubt. And so everyone opted for distraction. Everyone except Charlie.

Charlie stood, transfixed, at the window. She watched his hulking frame make its way down the steps across the street. From that distance, Charlie couldn't make out his face, and she was grateful for it. Just imagining him smug boiled her blood. Vince reached a car and pulled the door open. He paused and scanned his surroundings as if looking for something. Vince tilted his head up in her direction. Charlie planted her feet, squaring her shoulders. Her lips set in a thin line. She knew he couldn't see her. She also knew it didn't matter. He knew she was watching.

The knot in her stomach tightened. Releasing him was the right thing to do. They had so little on him and, asshole or not, he still had rights. Somehow, watching his car pull away felt criminal.

TIP #18

AN ORGANIZED LIFE IS A CALMER LIFE

Get your chickens in order and don't count your ducks before they hatch.

CHAPTER 38

"So we started in Washington?" Stef brought a pile of clothes over to the bed.

"Yup," Liam bit into an apple. He rested his feet on his luggage, having packed earlier.

"And we're about to dock in California."

"Uh huh," he managed between chews. Liam wrinkled his nose at her rushed folding.

"We've been at sea for close to three months."

"What are you getting at?"

"You know the drive would be like seventeen hours?" Liam rolled his eyes as she continued, "Apparently, people sail this distance in like a week. I get that we made loads of stops, but does this thing even have a motor?"

Liam walked up behind her and pushed the apple in front of her face. She took a large bite, wiping at the sides of her mouth with her index finger.

"Just saying," she bit the chunk into smaller pieces she could talk through. "It seems like an inefficient way to travel."

Liam reached down to organize her clothes by type.

"Think of it this way," he said, folding another shirt onto the appropriate pile. "We left no paper trail. There's literally no way to trace us. We're completely off the map."

"You can say that again."

A couple of hours after sunset, they looked over the marina, waiting to disembark. The bright San Diego Liam had expected stood artificially illuminated before them. It was just another city. Liam breathed easier

165

looking out hopefully at the traffic. There were more cars than he'd seen in a while. It wasn't overly noisy or crowded, but they would still be able to hide in the midst of it. Through the movement, Liam tuned into Stef's silence.

"You alright?"

"It's cold."

Liam laughed. "You remember Chicago, right?"

"Bite me," she hid her hands under her arms. "This is California, it's not supposed to be cold."

Liam pulled her case to the side and wrapped his arms around her.

"But what do you think? Could this be home?"

"It's cold, we know no one here, and we're barely employed. Feels like home."

In the Sutherlands' driveway the next morning, they loaded an old Jeep with boxes from the boat. After eating the large lunch May insisted on, they set off to a halted development on the outskirts of town.

The sun glinted off the exposed windows of abandoned buildings not covered by newspapers. A number of "for lease" signs guided their way out of the city. Liam pulled into the development Chris had mentioned. Conveniently half an hour out of the city, Bela Vista was meant to be an upscale residential complex that was deserted halfway through construction. Only a few houses were hospitable, giving them little choice; but the appeal of privacy and affordable accommodation was too good to pass up.

Liam drove them up a dirt road surrounded by sandy dunes. The tires crunched over gravel where he parked. Killing the engine brought on total silence. Liam rounded the car to where Stef stood taking in their surroundings. Thick hedges overflowing with deep pink flowers climbed the walls of the white house. They dragged their suitcases up the stone, careful to keep the wheels away from tearing up the grass.

Once all the boxes had been brought in from the car, hand in hand they walked the perimeter, settling on the sea facing hill. It was too far to hear the waves, though they could see them crash on the shore. Within minutes, the lively sky outshined the jeweled azure below. Pink stretched across the horizon darkening to purple before losing all color. It was too late in the year for stray lightning bugs to illuminate the night. Lights from the city twinkled in the distance competing with a smattering of stars overhead. Liam felt Stef shiver beside him. He looked her over questioningly. Still looking out, she lay her head on his shoulder.

"Just a little longer," she said melodiously.

He hummed and turned his gaze back out.

CHAPTER 39

L iam remained in the dark about how exactly Stef filled her days, but watching her return with a smile and groceries kept him happy. When she came back with news of a job and handfuls of paperwork, he started asking questions.

With the summer help gone back to school, Stef found a part time position at the local library. The pay was meager. The building and its patrons were getting on in their years. But, Stef enthusiastically explained, it afforded them a unique opportunity when it came to finding new names.

"Don't think of it as identity theft. It's more like sharing."

"Sharing?" Liam raised an eyebrow curiously. He had no plans on arguing with her. It amused him to see her flustered.

"We get 'legit' paperwork so we can live like normal people. We won't make any insane purchases. If possible, we can even improve their credit score. Besides, the library is so full of the really elderly; if we're smart about it, they'll never catch on."

Liam pondered her words. "How do you plan on getting their information? You any good with hacking?"

"Nah, I'm old school," she replied, smirking. "I was just going to eavesdrop."

"They just volunteer this information willingly?"

"Book people are trustworthy. We'd never be suspected of shady business."

Liam nodded, impressed. "You're an evil genius."

"I know," Stef shrugged. "At least I'm nice about it."

As someone who spent most of his life obsessing over the things he needed to get or do, Liam had a talent for noticing what wasn't there. However, in his contentment, he failed to note how Stef had stopped rolling her neck or how his fidgeting had decreased. The lack of furnishings did not bother Liam. He was too caught up in a job he actually enjoyed. Receiving steady payments distracted from the loss of government protection.

Even the tension between he and Stef was gone, not that there was much room for anything between them anymore. Feelings that they used to swallow circled them and warmed their space. They didn't choke on unspoken words. They braved arguments for a moment of discomfort that bred peace of mind by the time they fell asleep in each other's arms. Liam woke to Stef untangling herself from his limbs, to which he retaliated by pushing her back into the mattress. After watching her make her way into the shower with the stride of a well-loved woman, he would drift back off.

Hours later, Liam watched a figure bob past the flowered bushes. He got up from his avalanche of papers to meet Stef in the kitchen. He pulled items out of the canvas grocery bags she set on the table while she regaled him with tales of the library's visitors. Liam nodded along, keeping a close eye on the movements of the knife in his hand. Water rushed from the faucet behind him then quickly stopped. A gentle clang of metal on metal told him that she reached the stove. With a couple of beeps, Stef set the water to boil. She crossed the kitchen and pulled herself onto the counter beside Liam. He kept his eyes on the mixed vegetables in front of him. Stef twisted the cap off a bottle with a wet hiss.

"Play some music," she asked, taking a shallow sip.

Liam grabbed his laptop off the table and logged back into his account. They fell into a rhythm with the music that filled the kitchen.

"I spoke to Chris today."

"Oh?"

Trying to remain off the radar, Liam avoided using his phone, opting to walk to the nearest public phone.

"He mentioned having another project for me after this one."

"That's good. Did you agree to it?"

His mouth set into a thin line as he focused on thinly slicing the carrots.

"Not yet. I don't know if it's a good idea."

Stef snuck a carrot off his chopping board. She had a good vantage of his face from where she sat. Liam felt her eyes and looked up. He dropped the knife and reached for her drink.

"I thought you liked Chris."

Liam shrugged. "I do. And he pays well."

She took another carrot. Her munching subsided and he still hadn't continued.

"I'm not seeing the problem. We've got cozy digs - for free, may I add. You got a job, I've got the gig at the library..."

"Do you think we should stay here?"

"For a while. Why not?"

"Because," Liam ran a hand through his hair. "Someone knows us here."

Stef scoffed.

"Okay, maybe they don't really *know* us. But they are aware of one of our past lives."

"People who barely spend any time on dry land."

Liam took another swig. He turned to lean his back against the counter.

"I just think that it would be better if we moved on as soon as this book is done. Somewhere no one knows any of our identities. We can take a new one from the library and just disappear."

Stef conceded. "Chris and May will be devastated."

Liam nodded sadly.

"You're way too comfortable burning bridges," she said, shoving him lightly.

"Saves me from jumping off them."

Liam set down the bottle and leaned in for a kiss. He felt her smile against his lips. A soft moan spurred him on. His hands slowly inched up her thighs settling just under the hem of her skirt.

"The stove is still on," she mumbled against his cheek.

"Mm-hmm." Liam nipped at her neck. Her hands lay flat against his chest. He stopped thinking she would push him away. Turning in her nails, Stef scratched hard enough he winced, feeling it through his shirt.

"Turn off the hob."

TIP #19

TAKE RESPONSIBILITY

Do bad things keep happening to you or are you making bad decisions?

CHAPTER 40

H ad Vince been more introspective he might have considered changing careers. It was bad enough being the butt of every joke, which bordered on workplace bullying, but getting left behind at bars while his colleagues barely looked for the asshole that framed him made for a toxic work environment.

It had been a couple of months since all charges were dropped and Vince was still moping. Not that anyone noticed. Other than a half-assed toast upon his release, his presence was barely acknowledged. Everything went back to business like nothing happened. Either they didn't see him or they didn't care. Even Vince couldn't believe them to be that unobservant.

Vince had a stupid look about him. He knew that much from the way people treated him. But he was observant. Vince prided himself on the little things he could pick up about people. Not that they wanted to hear about his observations or theories about life. His name was frequently accompanied by calls to shut up. Which is why he was surprised to receive so much flack for keeping quiet. True, the robbery went a little sideways, but Vince had the good sense to dip when the clerk activated the silent alarm. He couldn't see how it was his fault that the others got arrested. Sure, he could have warned them, but they also could have paid attention. They didn't and got caught. Here they didn't and let Andy live among them.

That rat. He lived and worked with them for God knows how long. They let him get away with murder, so Vince could only wonder what else he managed to get up to.

"If he stole from us, don't you think he'd be dead by now?"

For all they knew, he might be. Vince heard that they had squeezed the Fed for information. Though it got Vince released, it turned out to be a dead end, so all talk of Andy died with him. He was no longer of interest to anyone. Almost anyone.

Vince didn't think much of Nick's trophy wife. He hadn't met her before, and, after doing so, he couldn't see the appeal. She had a pretty face, but she was too pudgy for his liking. He wouldn't turn her out of bed, but he didn't see the effort of luring her into one. In short, Vince didn't find her interesting. Or he didn't until he mentioned Andy. She was subtle about it. Her permanently bored expression had turned him off at first, but soon it made frequent appearances in his periphery. She always seemed to be around if the topic was Andy. Being thought of as an idiot used to bother him more, but recent events taught him to keep his mouth shut. He learned there was an advantage to letting people think less of you. It was possible the little trophy wife thought the same.

That motherfucker. Vince had to hand it to him. Andy had a pair. These idiots really didn't pay attention.

CHAPTER 41

The greater good was a dreadful shade of gray. In its name, they arrested Vince, aiming to make a dent in the mob. Then, for the sake of justice, they released the bastard to wreak havoc on an unsuspecting public. Now, in the hopes of catching Andy and getting answers about Horne, Charlie sat helplessly still and watched Vince force a woman into a car. She had called it in but when the woman was identified as Nikola Mirković's wife, she was ordered to hang back and let the charges add up.

Armed with instructions to tail Vince, Charlie followed them across state lines, ignoring the badge that burned her through her clothing reminding her that she had jurisdiction to make an arrest and save the woman. It wouldn't be as long a sentence as they wanted, but one charge of kidnapping could put him away. Charlie gripped the wheel tightly. She breathed in the minty air freshener and rubbed her bare foot against the crumb-covered carpet. Anything to keep her imagination out of Mischa's shoes. She could put an end to her suffering, if only the powers that be hadn't deemed it a necessary evil.

The gnawing in her gut returned with a vengeance. All the greasy takeout wasn't helping.

CHAPTER 42

L ight gently pried Liam's eyes open. His failure to put up the curtains prevented him from snoozing through the world's largest and most natural alarm clock. The sheets had bunched at his waist and tangled around his thighs. Liam reached across the bed. His hand found only a cold pillow. Stef had already left for work. He had hoped to indulge in a moment of selfishness before they had to be proper grown ups. He closed his eyes and imagined the soft curve of her shoulders. He wanted to trace her velvet skin, leaving a trail of wet kisses up to her neck until she stirred. He shot up and into the shower. As comfortable as the fantasy was, it wouldn't be the same without her.

Water drops followed Liam to the kitchen. A quick shake by the sink showered the countertops, confirming that he was in need of a haircut. As the coffee percolated, Liam grabbed a banana, opened his laptop, and clicked on some music for company. No sound came out of the speakers. He stepped closer and tried again to the same result. Liam took a seat, pulling the machine closer. The settings folder showed no connectivity issues. A prompt appeared in the music app, notifying him that another device was already in use. Liam thought of the phone at his bedside with a furrowed brow. He hadn't logged into his accounts on that phone. He couldn't if he wanted to. Fear of being traced made Liam throw his fancy twenty-first century brick into the Pacific and replace it with something that could barely handle texting. Knowing that Stef preferred an alternative streaming service, Liam wracked his brain for what other device he could be logged into.

The unpeeled fruit lay forgotten on the table. The coffee had finished brewing behind him. Liam no longer needed it. His heart beat violently in his chest. The mouse on the screen twitched over the second device logged into his account. Liam's mouth dried reading his own name. He had done it this time. All that effort to disappear and his own carelessness brought a murdered right to them. Liam used to joke that he would rather die than lose his music collection. By accessing his account he had signed his death sentence.

Ignoring the clatter of the chair he knocked over, Liam raced to his room to find his phone. He found a number of missed calls from her. He frantically dialed Stef, cursing each time the call went directly to voicemail. His thumbs raced across the screen sending message after message. The typos increased with his urgency and pacing back to the kitchen. Grammar be damned when their lives were on the line.

Here lies Liam No-Name, a first class idiot who endangered himself and his love over a playlist.

Liam considered calling the police. He got as far as the second number before his brain went blank. How would he even explain it to them? *'Hello, 911? I was in witness protection for accusing a guy of murder but now I'm not because I ran away. Well, he found me. Please help!'* He didn't have a name or location, just a vague description. Liam leaned over the computer and clicked on the other device. Under his breath he prayed it was just a fluke. The last login was thirty minutes ago. Liam looked up the address and the blood froze in his veins. The public library. Tears blurred his vision as he tried Stef's phone again. The call was quickly disconnected. He sobbed. A loud bell drew his attention back to the screen. There was a new message.

TIP #20

GET SOME EXERCISE

Make time for squats and cardio. You never know when you're going to need to duck and run.

CHAPTER 43

RUN

That's all the message said. But if she could text, then she must be safe. The thought repeated as Liam bolted out of their house. If she could text she must be safe and can get help. He just needed to find a place to hide until she could return.

The space was too open for his liking. The contractor didn't have the decency to leave some materials to hide behind or tools to use as a weapon. Most of the houses were too unfinished to provide any cover. Liam ran into a partially furnished show home. A sigh of relief got lost in his panting. Liam raced to the stairs but quickly reconsidered. The ground floor was a safer option. Although he didn't see himself getting through the day, he hoped to minimize injury in case he had to jump out of a window.

The end of the hall held the master bedroom that contained nothing but a bed frame covered by a dusty, moth-eaten quilt. Halfway between the window and the door, it seemed like a better option than the walk in closet. Either way, he felt like a trapped mouse, but he was better off avoiding the obvious dead ends. Crawling under the bed, Liam scolded himself for thinking the 'd' word. All he had to do was stay there and wait for Stef. Because she was fine. She sent a text, she was fine. And he would be too, if he just stayed there and waited. Easy enough.

Somewhere in the house a door blew closed. His denial ramped into overdrive, considering anything else the sound could have been. None of those options also covered the distinct sound of footsteps. Liam became conscious of his breathing. He held his breath, willing his heart to quiet.

When the footsteps disappeared he slid out from under the bed. The legs scratched against the hardwood floor. Liam watched the door with wide eyes. He waited a moment. Hearing nothing, he crossed the room and slowly unlatched the window. A piercing cry stopped him halfway out.

Liam tried to calculate the probability that it was a bluff. Perhaps a recording or maybe even someone else. He never excelled at math and the chance that it could be Stef sent him hurtling out the door. Liam ran into an outstretched hand holding a phone. The psycho wasn't as tall as he remembered, but he was certainly stronger than he thought. Liam didn't look away from the phone in time to see the fist heading for his jaw.

TIP #21

KISS

Cite Occam, cite Holmes; just keep it simple.

CHAPTER 44

C harlie had too much time to think. Sam didn't stick to a schedule when calling for updates and she had run out of ways to respectfully convey that she was still sitting in a filthy rental, watching a deviant manhandle some poor woman across the country so that they could secure a conviction against two suspected murderers over a year after she had tried to point out the inconsistencies.

It was glaringly obvious that they had handled the case all wrong. They had relied entirely on the word of some unemployed, woefully indebted kid who had disappeared from their protection, but not before withdrawing a considerable amount of their relocation fund. If he had run away, he would be disqualified as a witness. Charlie couldn't fault him for that. Andrija was a dangerous man. Liam would have done well to run away.

The facts seemed simultaneously true and false. It wasn't until she removed the witness from the mix did the narrative make more sense.

a murder took place;

there were two clear suspects, both had motive and opportunity;

another nearly identical murder occurred some time later;

one of the previous suspects could not have done it;

the other one, once again, had motive and opportunity.

It was possible that the stars had aligned for Liam, but Charlie didn't believe in fate, and she didn't like to give celestial bodies credit for human stupidity. However, she had to admit, if he was still alive, Liam Broci was the luckiest son a bitch.

TIP #22

DON'T EXPECT TO GET LUCKY

Luck is a finite resource, just like Helium and deadbeat dads, it'll eventually run out.

CHAPTER 45

Liam was the unluckiest man alive. Coming into consciousness, he knew he would be wishing for death soon. His head ached and dripped with something he didn't need a mirror to confirm was blood. At least he hoped it was blood; he didn't fancy his chances with brain fluid running down his face. Liam inhaled deeply, causing a coughing fit. His hands were, surprisingly, untied. He winced touching his throbbing nose, which sent an exploding pain up the back of his neck and all through his head. Liam opened his eyes a little. A pair of wrinkled jeans stood before him. He looked up through squinted eyes and immediately regretted the decision.

His body fell back into the seat. Liam's eyes watered violently. He reached up to cover his face. Another mistake, as it left his chest exposed. A hard hit to his lungs left Liam aggressively gasping for breath. The assault stopped.

"Now, you're going to tell me what you know."

"Huh?"

The man stepped closer. Light gleamed off the steel in his hands.

"No, no, no, no. Please!"

"What do you know," the psycho — whose name Liam had forgotten — asked, laying the blade against Liam's arm.

"I don't know what you mean," Liam cried. He screamed as the knife slid slowly against his skin. He pleaded again.

"I'm not going to ask you again."

"I don't know what I know!"

The man stood up grabbing Liam by the back of the head.

"Do not fuck with me right now," he gritted.

"I'm not," Liam sobbed. "It's a problem. I don't know what I know in general. You have to be more specific."

The man let go of his head and stalked off. Liam wiped away the trickle of blood and cradled his arm. He should keep quiet. It was the safest choice. Every time he had opened his mouth lately only led to trouble. The man headed to the door. As much as Liam wanted him to leave, without knowing where Stef was, he had to keep him in the room.

"You're with that Serbian mob, right?"

The man stopped by the door. He didn't turn around but Liam saw him peer over his shoulder back at him.

"Would it be foolish to hope that you're the forgive-and-forget type of mobster?"

Heavy items were set down slowly on a wooden table. The man blocked his view, so Liam tried to stretch. He groaned at the sharp ache around his ribs.

"You talk a lot for a man in your situation." His tone was even, but almost amused.

"I thought you wanted me to talk."

The man turned quickly.

"Sorry, sorry." Liam held his hands up. "I just got a lot of thoughts right now."

The man regarded Liam carefully. The way his ice blue eyes looked him over added to Liam's discomfort. He hunched over, shielding himself from view.

"Regret?"

Liam snickered. "That's not new."

The man narrowed his eyes. Liam winced, trying to remember his name. It started with an A, he was sure of it. Something scraped along the table. Liam looked up as the man approached with pliers in hand.

"No, come on. Adam! It's Adam right?"

His large palm collided with Liam's face. Disoriented, Liam couldn't figure out if that meant he got it wrong. His other cheek burned as he got struck again. Liam brought his arms up again.

"You made life impossible for me." The man — Andrew? — said, finishing his strike.

Liam yelled, "I make life impossible for myself."

"You ruined an innocent man's life."

"Bit of a stretch to call yourself innocent."

Andrew grabbed Liam's arm, and twisted. There was an audible pop. Liam yelled. Still holding Liam's arm, the man opened the pliers in his free hand.

"Okay, okay. I'm sorry!" Liam used his bleeding arm to pull away. "But come on, Andrew. How is what I did any different from what you do?"

Andrew pulled Liam in by the face. Standing a hair's breadth away, his hot breath tickled Liam's tender nose.

"It's Andy."

Liam whimpered. Knowing his name somehow made it worse. Andy stepped away again.

"How did you know I killed Dom?"

Liam tried not to expose his ignorance.

"Good guess?" He chuckled.

Andy knitted his brow. "You were lying?"

Liam nodded. The room went quiet. He looked up to find Andy watching him intently again with something Liam hoped was respect. At least he could take that to the grave.

Andy set the pliers down on the table, pushed a gun forward, and picked up the knife. He moved around the table to the end farthest from the door, never taking his eyes off Liam. The rule was unspoken. Liam had a chance to run.

Liam remained seated. The door was wide open. If he was fast enough he could run out. Maybe even grab the gun on the way. But he didn't know where Stef was. Liam still wasn't sure if Andy even had her. But the longer Liam kept him in that room, the safer she was. He looked back up, defeat clear in his eyes. Andy's features hardened. He motioned to the door but Liam shook his head. Tears prickled his eyes. Liam tried desperately to blink them back. Instead he lowered his head to accept his fate.

Andy stormed over and dragged him off the chair. On his knees, Liam looked up at Andy. There was no gloating, no triumph or victory to be found in his eyes. Only fury. Liam clenched his jaw and watched as Andy raised the knife to his throat. He closed his eyes and swallowed.

"So this is what you get up to when you're alone."

Liam's eyes shot open. He recognized that voice. The knife clangored by his feet. Clearly so did Andy.

TIP #23

DON'T CHASE HIM

There is crazy in love, then there's just plain crazy.

CHAPTER 46

S tef hoped that Liam would have had the sense to run, but a scream inside the house told her otherwise. Hiding under an open window, Stef dialed the police. Above, Liam whimpered. She disconnected the call. They needed help but it was too much of a risk. The police sirens would alert the man and force him to act rashly. She needed to find a way in. One that wouldn't get her or Liam killed.

Stef had been stocking shelves when she spotted an unattended laptop on the long pine table to her right. There was very little foot traffic at that time, so she wasn't concerned about its safety. Bright stickers arranged familiarly on the cover caught her eye. Stef set her books back down on the cart and walked closer to the computer. A tall man rounded the corner, wiping his hands on his jeans. Stef darted back into the shelves. She knew that computer. She definitely knew that face. Not wanting to attract his attention, she cowered further into the shadows, carefully keeping him in her sight.

The man stood with his back to her, faintly rustling something on the desk. Stef yelped as her back pocket vibrated. She pressed herself against the shelf out of his sight, sure that he had heard her. The corner of her phone vibrated loudly against the metal shelf. Stef took off before he could make his way down the aisle.

Not daring to look back, Stef ran out to the parking lot. She was glad to see there were no cars parked beside her. Staying low, she made her way into her car and locked the doors. She peered over the steering wheel, making sure she could see the exit. Stef cursed the designer of women's jeans for making the fabric lie so flat against her curves, leaving her no room to reach her phone. She fumbled with her phone but refused to take her eyes off the door. Gripping it tightly with two fingers, Stef finally managed to slide out her phone. It rang in her ear. "Come on, come on," she muttered to herself hoping Liam would just pick up. She glanced at the car clock. They had never bothered to set the correct time on it, but she was sure that he was already awake. She hung up and tried again, swatting away the tears from her cheeks.

The door to the library opened. The man stepped out. He crossed the parking lot in her direction. Stef ducked, sending the phone into the crevice between the seat and the center console. She cursed, sinking further into her seat. An engine started somewhere across from her. Stef stayed low. Through the driver's side window, she watched a small gray car drive past. Forgetting her phone, Stef scrambled with her keys. She inserted it into the ignition and slowly pulled out to follow him.

Stef crept in through the back door, past the granite countertops. The door to the next room was slightly ajar. She could hear the voices more clearly. Her lip quivered as Liam let out another painful scream. Stef tried to find relief in the noise. If he could scream, then he was still alive. It didn't give her any comfort.

A tall narrow door stood unvarnished across the room. Hoping it led around the adjacent room, Stef crawled past the open door. The smooth texture of her jeans slid on the black and white tiles. She turned to press her back against the wall to continue facing the room. Stef slid a hand up the rough door to reach the handle. Opening it just a crack revealed a pantry. She backed into it then turned onto her hands and knees. Once her body no longer propped open the surprisingly heavy door, it swung shut. Stef scrambled into a corner and waited. She stood cautiously. A pained yelp could be faintly heard through the thick walls. Stef made her way back to the door only to find it lacked a handle on the inside. She grabbed at the bevels, hoping to gain purchase and pull the door open. There was no use in throwing herself at it, as it opened inward. Stef busied herself climbing the shelves to reach the frosted glass pane above the door. She was a few inches short of reaching the lock. Stretching further jostled a loose shelf beneath her feet.

Stef settled back on the ground. It had become too silent. Pressing herself against the door, she searched for any sign of life. Her racing heart drowned out any mumbling and got louder. She stepped back into the corner as the thuds turned into heavy footsteps. Stomps crossed the tiles in her direction, unevenly as though from different feet. Light filled the pantry. Before she had the chance to adopt a fighting stance, someone fell and the door slammed shut once again.

The new prisoner sobbed on the floor, slowly dragging itself into a sitting position. The little light from the frosted glass showed the petite frame of a terrified woman. She didn't appear to be armed. Her hair fell back as she adjusted, revealing a horrendous bruise on her face. Though it wasn't safe to say anything for certain, Stef was pretty sure the woman didn't pose a threat.

"Can you get up?"

The woman's head whipped in Stef's direction. Her bulging eyes brimmed with tears and surprise.

"Who are you?"

Stef crossed her arms. "I was here first. Who are you?"

They took turns blinking at each other. Nervous energy filled the now crowded space.

"Have you seen Andy?" The woman's voice trembled. Stef opened her mouth to speak but promptly closed it. Something about the way she asked bothered Stef. She was speaking from concern, not fear. Andy must not have been the one that threw her in. Stef's mind raced with more questions than before. She froze in horror as one thing became clear: there was more than one of them out there. If she thought they were in deep shit before...

Stef straightened up. There was no time to waste.

"Can you stand?" She asked more forcefully.

The woman on the floor nodded. She grabbed the lower shelves for balance and slowly lifted herself. She groaned in pain. Stef wanted to help her up. Apprehension kept her in place. The woman stood, still holding onto the shelves.

"We need to get out of here." Stef pointed to the glade pane above them. "I think that window opens, but I couldn't reach it on my own."

The woman followed Stef's finger and nodded. She was shorter than Stef, but not by much. Between her injuries and stature, Stef figured it would be safer if she did the heavy lifting herself.

"Get on my shoulders and see if you can open it."

The woman sniffled but complied without question. Stef kneeled and grabbed the woman's legs. Wobbling slightly, she stood, holding on tighter. Keeping one hand on the top shelf, the woman fiddled with the latch. The glass swung out into the kitchen.

"Got it."

Her voice was still quiet, but Stef could make out a hint of an accent. Given the circumstances, Stef assumed eastern European, making it more likely she ran with the crowd Stef was trying to run away from.

"Good. Climb through and open the door from the outside."

"I can't," she wailed, clamoring down.

The woman began to cry again, more loudly this time. Stef moved closer with outstretched arms. The woman looked her way and cowered. Stef backed off quickly keeping her hands visible. Going off that reaction and bruise, she had probably been slapped around plenty.

"I'm sorry," Stef gently placed her hands on the woman's shoulders. "But we really need to get out of here."

The woman continued to sob on the floor. Stef looked around the room again, hoping something new had appeared on the empty shelves.

"What's your name?"

"Mischa," she blubbered.

"I'm Frankie," Stef said the only name that came to mind. "How do you know Andy?"

Mischa chewed her lip. "We're together."

Noting her hesitation, Stef recoiled. Mischa's eyes widened.

"Why? What's wrong?"

Stef paused. "How long have you been together?"

Mischa awkwardly stood up.

"A while," she said forcefully. She puckered her lips. "How do you know Andy?"

Stef bit her lip as Mischa had done earlier. She looked away dramatically and faked a sob. Softly she whispered into the corner, "He told me he loved me."

Stef didn't turn immediately. She wiped at her nose to steal a glance at the woman. In the dim light, her face reddened.

"Get me up there."

Stef kept her head down as she lowered herself. She smirked, glad Mischa couldn't see her face from the top of her shoulders. Watching her climb out of the window, Stef swallowed hard. She wiped her face as the door opened from the outside.

"Let's go find Andy."

CHAPTER 47

He got him. With no support or faith from his peers, he did it. They had tried and failed. Even killed a Fed and didn't come close. But he didn't. Vince suffered in jail and drove across the country but it was worth it to catch Andy with his pants down — or as good as judging by the guy on his knees.

Vince was too pleased to be offended by the shock on Andy's face.

"What?" he gloated. "You didn't think I'd find you?"

Andy unhanded the man who crumpled onto the floor. He stood to full height. His face set like stone. Vince stood in place squaring his round shoulders.

"How did you find me?"

Vince reached for his pants. Andy gripped his blade tightly taking a step closer. Vince threw a hand up mockingly and pulled out his phone. He pressed the screen and smirked as Andy's phone rang on the table. Andy watched it ring until Vince disconnected the call.

"No one knows this number." He shifted, keeping his grip on the knife.

Vince threw his head back. "Is that what you call her?" he guffawed. "Interesting nickname."

Andy stilled. His nostrils flared. Vince swelled with pride knowing he got under the pretty boy's skin. Andy's eyes shifted quickly to Vince's side. He turned to look at the table and laughed again. Lying beside the phone was Andy's gun.

Vince shook his head laughing. And people thought he was the dumb one? It was almost too easy. Vince knocked it off the table with a smirk. He didn't bother unholstering his own. Stepping forward Vince flexed his hands. He wanted to enjoy destroying that pretty face.

CHAPTER 48

Mischa looked positively murderous. Stef feared she might have overdone it.

"Wait, would you stop?" Stef grabbed Mischa's wrist. "We can't just barge in there. They have guns!"

"Fine," she said, pulling free from Stef's grasp. "Let's get our own." Mischa darted out the backdoor to a car parked haphazardly over the cobbled path. Stef didn't follow her out. She searched the kitchen for something to help. Under the sink Stef found a purple bucket and a bottle of bleach. Remembering an article she had read a while back about dangerous cleaning mistakes, she rummaged the cabinets for vinegar with no luck. Each one was emptier than the last. Through the window over the sink Stef saw flashing lights crawling past at a distance. If only she could get their attention. Stef shifted her search for something loud. Sighing in resignation, she headed outside to the car. Perhaps a gun was the way to go.

Mischa had vanished. The car sat with its doors thrown open. Stef rooted around the vehicle. There was no trace of any weapon. If there were one, Mischa had probably already taken it. Looking at the front seat, Stef considered laying on the horn. She dismissed the thought and went around the back to the trunk. Stef crossed her fingers for a crowbar at the very least. The little button underneath was stuck. Using all her strength, Stef struggled to lift the cover. Frustrated, she struck the car just over the license plate. The trunk popped open. She jumped excitedly then pulled it up. Bits of trash covered the fabric. Stef leaned in then immediately drew back at the smell. Spoiled food and who knows what else wafted out. She gagged. Covering her nose in the crook of her elbow, Stef leaned back in. Among the chaos, Stef found a box of ammo turned on its side. It jingled as she shook it. That would have to do.

Back inside the kitchen, Stef pulled a hollow frying pan out of the oven. Setting it on top, Stef prayed they had connected the gas line as she poured in the bullets. She turned the knob, satisfied at the hiss coming out of the hob. Stef set a lit match until a blue flame circled the burner. Staying low, she ran back out of the house.

Stef crouched over to her original hiding place under the window. Slowly she peered over the ledge. She could see two men standing by the exit. The one with his back to her blocked the other. Stef stood a little straighter, searching the floor for Liam. He was slumped over in the center of the room. She waved frantically to get his attention. Stef tapped quietly on the laminated panel. Liam raised his head. His teary eyes widened at her. She couldn't stop the smile that broke out over her face. Stef signaled for him to wait then blocked her ears with her fingers. She hoped he would get the hint from that.

Stef crouched in the gravel. Through her pants she could feel the pebbles embedded in her knees and calves. Tempted to rise to check on the situation, Stef threw herself back down as loud pops exploded behind her. Assuming the risk, Stef stood quickly and reached into the window. Liam was too far to pull through. He kept crawling towards her as the pops continued to shoot off around him. A large mass collapsed, narrowly missing him. Liam froze in place. Stef watched Andy lean over the larger man's body then collapsed on the floor. The noise died down inside the house. Stef held her breath and waited. Two gunshots killed the silence.

TIP #24

FACE THE MUSIC

If you fuck up, own up to it.

CHAPTER 49

It was ruined. Standing in between Vince at the door and the pathetic kid at his feet, Andy wondered how it all went so wrong. He was just about to fix everything when that lumbering idiot burst through the door. Andy resisted the urge to kick the whimpering asshole. He would come back for him with no interruptions.

Vince swiped at Andy who quickly side stepped him. Vince was bigger, but Andy suspected that he was faster. He just needed to keep some distance between them. Andy wrinkled his nose. The stench of body odor reached him where he stood. Andy shook his head in disgust. The idiot came all this way to kill him but couldn't even make himself presentable. Cold fury ran through his veins. Andy's face contorted beautifully with hatred. Vince stepped up to him swinging the logs he called arms. Andy dodged the jab to his face. Lunging forward with his knife, Andy caused Vince to take a step back. A blast from the kitchen stopped them both. Vince ran forward away from the explosion. Taking advantage of his inclined position, Andy caught Vince in the ribs. A kick to the knees knocked him face first to the ground. Andy grabbed the gun from the back of Vince's trousers. He tried to turn but Andy's foot kept him down.

Pop.

Pop.

Andy spitefully kicked Vince's body. He had fallen just beside the kid who curled up. Andy looked him over. He was too tired to continue playing. He lifted the gun and took aim.

"Andrija?"

Andy was a man of faith but he was beginning to think God had abandoned him. Frustrated, he groaned, not sure how much more he could take. Andy turned around slowly. Mischa stood in the doorway pointing a gun at him. The spot on the floor where it had been was empty. Andy rolled his eyes.

"Petal, put that down."

Her hands shook but she kept the barrel trained on him.

"Baby, I'm not in the mood for this. Put the gun down."

His hand twitched. Her eyes widened and she tightened her grip, sliding her finger over the trigger. Andy exhaled loudly. He made a show of putting his gun away.

"Mischa," he treaded lightly towards her. "My love."

"Your love?" Her voice stopped him. It held neither the anger he expected nor the passion he was used to. She was too calm. "You left me and now you call me your love?"

Blood rushed in his ears.

"Mischa…"

"Shut up!"

He narrowed his eyes at her. He could close the distance between them before she had a chance to shoot. Andy doubted that she even knew how to use it. As if reading his thoughts, Mischa unlocked the safety.

"Now you are going to answer. Is there someone else?"

Andy tensed but stayed put. He softened his tone again. "Petal."

"Don't even try to lie to me right now," she screamed, jabbing the weapon in his direction. Andy held his hands up.

"I didn't say anything."

"Then say something." She sniffed. "Why did you leave me?"

"I had to."

"Why," she wailed.

Andy rubbed his neck. She was exhausting. "It all happened so fast. I just had to go."

"But you killed him. Vince told me."

"And you believed him," Andy asked, raising his voice.

"Why would he lie?"

"To turn you against me." Andy gestured between them. "And clearly it worked." Andy took a small step back turning away from her slightly. "How long did it take him to convince you? Or," he paused, "did you replace me with him."

She took an angry pace forward then stopped. "You think I'm stupid, Andrija? You disappeared and said nothing. I know about the other girl. Who is she?"

Andy threw his hands up. "Who?"

Mischa lowered the barrel to his crotch.

"Who is she?"

"Stop pointing that thing at me."

She tilted her head, curling her finger around the trigger.

"Mischa, I'm fucking warning you."

Holding her position, she quirked an eyebrow, silently repeating the question.

"Point that thing away from my cock," he bellowed.

"Then tell me who she is."

"WHO?"

"The girl in the closet!"

Andy remembered his surroundings. A movement caught his eye. The kid had dragged himself across the room to another door. A pair of arms extended through the opening. They nearly reached him. Andy pulled his gun back out and fired towards the door. A shot and a scream pulled him in opposite directions. Tight pressure filled him. He couldn't hear anything more over the buzzing pain that radiated from his chest. Andy turned back to Mischa who ran across the room to him. There was shock in her electric blue eyes. He watched the gun fall out of his hand. His shirt felt wet. Andy ran a finger over the buttons of his shirt until they skipped one. Lifting them to his face they were doused in red. Andy dropped to his knees muttering.

"Forgive me f-."

CHAPTER 50

L iam used all his strength to look unconscious. He kept himself tense to stop from visibly flinching at the execution that took place far too close for comfort. Lifting only his eyes, Liam could make out a large heap on the floor. Though he never got to see his face, Liam had a pretty good idea who was lying beside him, emitting the foul smell that kept him awake.

A voice in the doorway distracted Andy. Liam quietly shuffled away from the dead body. Just over its head, he watched the front door open. Content that Andy was no longer paying him any attention, Liam continued scooting around the body. He managed to get perpendicular when Andy turned in his direction. Liam squeezed his eyes shut. The hem of Andy's pants brushed his arm. He pulled it closer. The argument continued above him.

The door opened further. Liam scooted towards it until his chest constricted. He struggled to catch his breath. His body screamed in agony. Relaxing his muscles released a flood of pain that made him want to pass out. Liam dropped his head onto the cold floor. He wasn't going to make it.

The voices got louder. If ever there was a time to make a dash, that was it. Liam tried to get up. He suppressed a groan when his arm buckled underneath him. Andy stood almost directly in front of him. Through his legs, Liam saw the woman holding Andy's attention. As loud as they were, he couldn't make out what they were saying. He wasn't trying particularly hard to listen. All of his efforts went to scooting away from the lunatics.

It was so close. The overcast sky waited just beyond the door. If he stood, he could make it out in three steps. Liam huffed. Stef appeared in the bottom corner of the frame. Loose coils waved around her face as she motioned him over. Over his shoulder, the couple remained intently focused on each other: the woman on Andy's face, Andy on her gun. Breathing out through gritted teeth, Liam pushed himself forward. The gash stung each time he set down his arm. That was nothing compared to his shoulder. Each slide forward brought excruciating pain. Stef extended further into the room. Her fingers grazed his.

"Just a little more," she mouthed.

Liam sat up on his knees. Nearly there. He took a chance at the scream behind him, grabbing Stef's hands and hurtling out.

A deafening thrumming kept Liam from registering anything other than Stef's hands. He squeezed them. She tried to pull them down but he held firm. He was there. She was okay. Horror crossed her face. Liam loosened his grip and brought his hands to her cheek. He couldn't feel her skin under his fingertips. His whole body was strangely numb.

Pushed onto his back, Liam struggled to catch his breath. Stef appeared above him. Distraught tears flowed down her face. She called out, but he couldn't hear to whom. Movement blurred behind her. Everything sounded like he was underwater. Stef's face washed out in waves of blue and red.

Above, thick clouds began to part.

TIP #25

LEARN TO LET GO

Some fights aren't worth it.

CHAPTER 51

Charlie's hip rested on the reception desk. She drummed her fingers impatiently. A nurse on the phone eyed her disapprovingly. Charlie shoved her hands into her jacket pockets. The door to the patient rooms opened to let a family out. Charlie gave them a curt nod and headed down the pale corridor.

A woman strode in her direction, shaking a phone in her hand. Charlie stood against the wall to watch her pass. She looked just as she had in the video. Same thick braid slung over her shoulder. Same worried expression. When she turned the corner, Charlie approached the room she had just vacated.

There he lay. The last piece of the puzzle. Bruised, swollen, sporting a dislocated shoulder and a couple of broken ribs. He looked good for a man that spent a day with armed mobsters. Liam stirred. His lashes fluttered but his eyelids remained shut. Hoarsely he called out for Stef.

"She stepped out."

Liam opened his eyes. He held apprehension there. Grunting, he sat upright and scooted back into the pillows. Charlie pulled out her badge. He remained tense.

"You're a lucky man, Liam."

He groaned in disagreement.

"I can see why you wouldn't think so," she chuckled. "But if you knew half of what Andy was suspected of."

Liam's breath hitched. Charlie was sure that, somewhere in the hospital, his heart monitor spiked.

"He won't be bothering you," she said. "He was DOA by the time we showed up."

Charlie moved closer. She ran a hand over the blanket by his feet and felt Liam watching her intently.

"So you want to tell me what happened?"

He raised an eyebrow. "I think it's pretty obvious what happened."

"Sure looks that way doesn't it. Why don't you tell me all the same?"

Liam sighed deeply.

"He found us on the island. Andy," he added with a scowl. "So we ran. Couldn't reach Aquilino. Couldn't be sure we could trust him. So we ran." Liam cleared his throat. He adjusted himself to sit straighter. "Things were fine down here until he found us again. Well, me at least. But I thought he had Stef so I — well, he." Liam swallowed hard. Charlie walked over and poured him a cup of water from the pitcher at his bedside. He drank quickly. She refilled the cup. He took slower, more deliberate sips and thanked her.

"That's when the rest of them came." He set down the cup.

"Yup," Charlie nodded. "Lines up with what your girlfriend said."

Liam chewed the inside of his mouth.

"Anything else?"

He shook his head quickly.

Charlie considered him a moment. Her gut told her he wasn't telling the whole story. But from what she could see, the little he told was true. Even if he was a bit shifty, there was no proof he had actually done anything wrong. She had nothing to gain by trying to convince others that he had. The facts remained the same. The two suspects and most probable perpetrators were dead, so Dominic's case would likely go cold. Following her ordeal, Mischa was very talkative and Charlie's bosses were only too happy to listen, especially concerning Horne. They no longer needed Liam's testimony. As far as they could tell, he wasn't in danger. There was no need to jeopardize that.

Liam looked over her shoulder. Stefanie stood frozen in the doorway. Her chunky boots were surprisingly quiet; Charlie hadn't heard her approach. Charlie nodded politely at Liam, pulling something from her pocket. She passed Stef a card in her hand. Stef took it with a nod.

It wasn't ideal. The bad guys didn't get away, but they didn't get caught either. A part of her still wanted answers, but she knew the questions weren't worth asking. She had all the pieces but would never assemble this puzzle. Charlie could learn to live with that.

CHAPTER 51

S tef looked between the card in her hand and Liam who shrugged on the bed. She shook her head at him.

"You're an idiot."

"Hey, be nice. I got shot." He patted the space on the bed next to him.

"Because you're an idiot." She sat down tentatively. Liam raised his arm giving her more room. She nestled into the crook of his neck. Her hair brushed against his ear.

"Correlation doesn't imply causation."

Stef looked up through her lashes. "You don't think your stupidity led to the bullet in your back?"

Liam rolled his eyes.

"Where did you go?"

Stef toyed with the smooth edge of the blanket, careful not to apply any pressure on his chest.

"Was talking to Frankie." Liam laughed then winced. Stef shot up, looking him over worryingly. Liam shook his head and breathed out deeply. He made an attempt to smile comfortingly. She didn't look convinced. He tugged on her arm. She settled back down.

"I gave her an abridged version of the past year. She said they'd come down for a visit."

Liam huffed.

"She may have an ulterior motive," Stef smiled mischievously. "Said she needs someone to manage her blog." She lifted her chin to look at him directly. "It's yours if you want it."

"I think I'll pass."

They lay in silence for a moment.

"I think we should stick around here for a while," he said to the ceiling. He felt Stef nod. "They said that no one will look for us, but they also can't be sure how much they know about us."

Stef laced her fingers with his.

"Besides, I still need to finish up this book."

"Good," Stef sighed. "I may have a project to look into."

Liam pulled back to see her face.

"Just a little something to help people who want to escape for whatever reason. Not everyone qualifies for witness protection, you know? And I don't know about you but I think I got pretty good at sorting out those little details."

Liam chuckled. "If you ever need to write an instruction guide or something, I may know a guy."

Acknowledgements

I'd like to start off by thanking my parents who weren't the least bit surprised when I told them I had written a book. I suppose they saw it coming, between the weekend trips to the library with dad and every time mom turned a blind eye to me sneaking in new books during my rebellious youth. I also thank my sisters for not ratting me out.

There are a number of supportive people who have talked me off the proverbial ledge. However too many of them have such long names writing them all out will be a novel in itself so here I go.

Niyati. This would not have happened without you. The potential you saw in the stories I passed you in class led to this.

Max and Nicole, for a couple who appreciate my humor I can't thank you enough for hearing my ideas and believing in them even when I tried to pass them off as jokes.

Samantha and Yolanda, you two have been excellent sounding boards throughout all of this. Thursday nights were healing.

Thank you, Ciaran, for nipping my whining in the bud and snapping me back to focus.

Matt, I guess I have no choice but to thank you for pestering me into picking up my pencil. It's like you had a sensor for when it had been still for too long.

And Jen. Jenny. Genevieve. It's impossible to stay in a slump when someone as cool as you motivates me to keep moving forward.

Social media has put me in contact with such interesting characters, some of whom have shown appreciation for my writing. To them, I am so grateful as those comments and messages fueled me.

Finally, I would like to extend a huge thank you to the team at City Limits Publishing for taking a chance on me. Robert Martin, you've been a fantastic point of contact. Thank you for working around my strange hours and ever changing addresses. I can only apologize to Lilly Peterson for my numerous typos and excessive swearing. Working with your team has been an absolute dream.

About the Author

Ana Neimus was born when reality became too much for her alter-ego. Instead of using her law degree to practice the science of human stupidity, she builds stories around the conversations in her head.

MORE FROM CITY LIMITS PUBLISHING

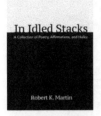

Six years of writings sat unfinished until COVID-19 gave Robert Martin the time needed to finish the job. *In Idled Stacks: A Collection of Poetry* provides a glimpse into the life and mind of the author. Featuring poetry about the Coronavirus pandemic, racial civil unrest, relationships, life's storms, and more, In Idled Stacks is an emotional and fascinating look into the life of the everyman.

Dances with Words, a collection of over 500 haiku speaks to the pathos, pain, and passion of this journey we call life. Random thoughts, rants, raves, reminiscences, prayers of praise, et al – framed in poetic bite-size bits – 17 syllables at a time. Built around song titles and lyrics, the writer weaves themes that touch the deepest part of us. Love, God's love, forgiveness, tears, sadness, healing and loss – et al. My prayer is that my passion and pathos – my loves and losses can speak to you, wherever you are – whatever your story.

Poems of Political Protest: An Anthology is a collection of poems by various authors who are attempting to make their own waves in their community and in the global community. They're the words of the hurting, the fighting, and the driving force behind real and impactful change. All we have, all we own freely and clearly, are our words. May this collection bring about action.

Portraits of the Pen: A Collection of Short Stories features over two dozen short stories that paint glorious portraits of the characters within. From stories of life lessons to romance, suspense to fantasy, be taken away to many worlds where rich characters tell stories of the every man, and every woman. Watch time pass and romance blossom in The Beach House. Journey to Chalcey in the thriller Foundling. Learn a valuable life lesson in Paxton's Socks. Each piece has been hand picked and features layered stories that invoke strong senses and paint detailed pictures in the minds of the readers.

An emotionally scarred woman in 2019 gets the chance to go back in time to stop a terrible tragedy. But there's a catch: she must overcome her insecurities and learn to trust people — and herself — in order to save dozens of innocent lives. Brenda Lyne lives just outside Minneapolis, Minnesota with her two kids and two cats. *Charlie's Mirror* is her first novel, and she believes it is never too late to follow your dreams.